Beyond the Shadows

Beyond the Shadows, Volume 1

Shanna Robillard

Published by Shanna Robillard, 2021.

BEYOND THE SHADOWS

First edition. July 30, 2021.

Copyright © 2021 Shanna Robillard.

ISBN: 978-0578962672

Written by Shanna Robillard.

Table of Contents

Thank you to Kimmie, for always being a great sounding board and fabulous cousin;

To Meg for that little tweak to the title;

And to my husband for being the most supportive person in all facets of my life.

Also from the Author

Beyond the Shadows Trilogy

Beyond the Shadows
SpellCast from Darkness
Against the Coming Dark

The Brimstone Court Novels

Book One: The Darkest Echo
Book Two: Consumed in the Dark
Book Three: Burned in the Dark (Coming June 2025)
Book Four: Wanted in the Dark (Coming Summer/Fall 2025)
Book Five: Falling in the Dark (Coming Winter 2025)
Book Six: Wounded in the Dark (Coming Spring 2026)
Book Seven: Salvation in the Dark (Coming Summer 2026)

Standalone Books

A Tale by Moonlight
The Seven Lives of May Levesque
Queen of the High Seas
Folklore: The Beginning
Rising Phoenix

Prologue

He didn't know the cold of winter anymore.

Michael Hawkins knew that he looked absurd to the people passing him on the lane. Why, here was a grown man, walking around in a torn shirt and ragged pants in winter, yet he felt no chill? How could this man be immune from the stark, bone-cold of January? How were his feet and hands not black with frostbite? The intense stares from flabbergasted men and gasps of disgust from their delicate, feminine partners burned him like a brand.

How did he still have a flush to his cheeks?

It was true that Michael could not feel the icy fingers of Lady Winter caressing his skin. Frost did not seep into his bones. No, it was quite the opposite. The night was clear and bright in the light of the gibbous moon, shining like the sun and illuminating the doorways and carriages. Despite the lamplighters finishing their rounds and smoke rising from chimney stacks throughout the city, the brisk air felt fresh and clean. Hanging ice crystals sparkled in the moonlight like sand on the beach.

In fact, the snow crunching beneath Michael's feet felt like he had always imagined sand would feel, slipping between his toes. He had never been to a beach or a shore, knowing only the cobblestone and masonry of the city. Yet he pretended the seasons had changed positions and taken on the attributes of their counterparts. He felt as warm as if he strolled upon a Caribbean island shoreline—or at least what he thought it might be like. Truly, he felt...comfortable.

But those damn stares...

It was those stares that kept him from basking in it all: their disgust at his simple existence. Lord help them if he might come close enough to be in their orbit. Hopefully they wouldn't discover what he smelled like—those staring people—each of them giving him as wide a berth as possible, hoping to avoid him altogether.

He knew, though, what they were thinking; he recognized it in the looks they gave him. They saw the dirt on his face, the muck in his matted brown hair, the rips and stains on his shirt and pants. His countenance was disturbing to their delicate sensibilities, an affront to their very nature. He knew they would prefer to step on him rather than around him.

This is what came from having spent a month on the streets. He cringed inwardly, knowing he couldn't do anything to correct his appearance, that no one would ever let him get near. He also felt his anger rising, hating all of them for judging him while also knowing they were right.

"Dirty scavenger," whispered a man to his wife. Michael clenched his fists and hurriedly turned down an alley. His jaw clenched tight, he lowered himself down to sit behind a frozen rain barrel that was bulging with ice.

Yes, they were right. He was a dirty scavenger. He would feed on anything anyone would toss out of their kitchen, if it wasn't maggot-ridden. He would grasp and claw for scraps and leftover bits of offal from anywhere, taking whatever he could to survive. He would relish having it in his belly and having another day of life.

This was how he had lived each day. At least, before she came and showed him something else to scavenge for...

Was he bloodless? *Yes*, he mused, *I must be*. After all, he was sitting there, hunkered down behind the barrel of ice as soft snowflakes coated his eyelashes. There couldn't possibly be any blood left within him. Afterall, why else would he crave it so?

"She sucked it out of me like a damn leech," he muttered to himself. Clearly she had left him dry. Now he was wandering around a city of wintry alleys—alleys that felt like beaches—searching, thirsting, *hunting...*

The more Michael thought about it, the more miserable he became. Visibly scowling, he acknowledged that he hated himself: he hated what he had become, hated the strangers that stared at him, hated the sand-like snow under his feet—hated *her*. Only one thing could make the empty pain deep in his belly subside. He didn't want to desire it, didn't want the cravings, but the diabolical bitch had made him this way. Now he was a new kind of monster, one that he had never known existed, and he wished he'd never met her.

It was too late. He knew what he needed so desperately. She had told him he would develop a hunger for life, but he never knew—never thought—she meant *this*. Hell, he never thought he would need—

Michael's thoughts ceased, having become distracted by a corpulent, well-dressed man passing the alley entrance. Standing up, Michael crept to the front of the alley, rounding the corner and watching as the man turned into the inn next door. Scurrying to the glass front, Michael stared inside, spying on the rich fat man sitting at a table. He was already drinking the recently popular Stone Fence cocktail and waiting for his meal.

Something built silently within Michael's hollow frame as he stared. It was something dark, something hungry. While the snow fell from above, he watched the man, and he waited.

Wiping the drink from his mustache, the rich fat man smiled gleefully as a plate of pheasant was placed in front of him. Grasping his fork and knife, he deftly sliced into the pheasant's breast and speared a piece with his fork. He ate with gusto, juices dripping into his beard and slurping pheasant from his fork, thinking of nothing but consuming the roasted bird lying in front of him. The fat man ripped a hunk of crusty bread loaf and sopped up the juices, licking his fingers to get every delicious and tasty bit. He was going to clean the bird so well the cooks wouldn't be able to use the bones for soup! Grabbing his drink by a fat handle at its side, the man guzzled and slurped, clearly pleased with himself as much as his meal. Laughing aloud, either at some joke he remembered or sheer amusement, he returned to his plate and again attacked the half-eaten carcass atop it.

The man didn't see anyone staring at him from the snow. He was enjoying himself and this fantastic day he'd been having. He had sold a prized pistol in his shop to a gullible novice from out of town, reaping in three times the normal price! Shortly afterwards, he learned his shipment of handmade tobacco pipes ordered from Germany was arriving tomorrow—a full month ahead of schedule. Considering that his mistress had left him two weeks ago—and his wife a day after that—he had been in a foul mood and needed something uplifting to happen. This great news turned out to be just what he needed, and he chose to reward himself with a fine meal, determined to enjoy it immensely—and indeed he was! He thought he might go to the house of ill fame down the way and take in a private show after he was done, too. Why yes, that would be the makings of a grand day, wouldn't it?

Cheered by his brilliant idea for a celebration, this stinking, odious meatsack stood up, dropped his coin on the table for the meal, and walked to the door. Taking his coat and hat from the stand, he bundled up for his trek to the brothel. He didn't notice that anyone was watching him, though. He didn't notice the eyes out in the snow had gone.

Opening the door to the cold, the meatsack trod down the front steps and headed East along Smythe Street towards Phillipps Square. He knew the way easily enough, having been to the brothel several times, and he smiled thinking of the upcoming pleasures of the evening. Grinning like a buffoon and feeling near to bursting from his dirty thoughts, he adjusted himself as he walked. An elderly aristocrat strolled by with his two poodles, each growling as they warily watched the stranger walk by their master. The aristocrat made a sound of disgust, causing the meatsack to smirk in amusement and leer at the blue blood with an exaggerated expression of glee. With pleasure, he watched the elderly man cower and scurry away with his dogs, dragging them behind him. Laughing heartily, he turned his attention back towards his destination.

The meatsack loved to piss off the wealthy. It seemed to him that they never earned their money respectably—not like he did, anyway. Any chance he had, he helped them be on their guard and wary of their surroundings. *That's one more*, he thought. Continuing on toward his pleasurable evening, he had no inkling of being watched.

Michael was in the darkness, focused intently on the meatsack like a lion on a gazelle. He hid just to the side of an old shipping company office, cloaked in its shadows. His lips peeled back to reveal his teeth as he hissed in anger and hunger. He agreed that the wealthy were evil men, but he could tell by the attitude and demeanor of this wretched man that he was no better than they. Those that passed judgement were typically terrible judges of character to begin with, and they usually saw in others exactly what was wrong within themselves. While Michael never liked to judge anyone by their outward appearance, he needed what only a human could provide, and the meatsack didn't appear to be someone others would miss.

Considering his options, Michael chose to make his way around to the next alley only two blocks ahead. He scaled up to the second-story ledge, leaping and climbing the remainder of the building to reach its rooftop. He moved stealthily, slinking across the flat expanse of wood planks, quick and quiet. As if in a blur of silence, he was suddenly at the far edge of the roof, peering down to check for prying eyes before springing over to the next building. He landed, soft and silent, crouched down and motionless like a large predatory beast, as if expecting an attack to come lashing out of the darkness.

Michael did this for another three building rooftops until he had reached the last roof edge. Overlooking his destination, the alley of the candlemaker's shop, he jumped down and kept still, listening. Very shortly, he heard the heavy, shuffling footsteps of the meatsack. He quickly made his way to the dark border of the alleyway, cloaking himself in the black of night. His heightened sense of smell told him the man was close. Whispering softly like a breath on the wind, he spoke to him.

"This way... Come this way and find pleasure... Pleasure... Pleasure..."

The meatsack heard his call, stopping and turning to the alley just to his right. His arousal was piqued by something he heard in the voice. There was something in it he couldn't name but knew he wanted—he wanted it *urgently*. His mind clouded over, a sudden onrush of fog, blocking all normal and rational thought that would tell someone to run. His eyes glazed over, and he mumbled a hushed, "Yes." His posture relaxed, and he stumbled into the alleyway. Stepping into the darkness, it seemed to close around him, like coming into a lover's arms. The voice continued to call to him, and he walked further into the black depths of the corridor, his outward appearance belying the heart racing in his chest, loins tightening in reaction to the enthralling images of pleasure invading his brain. He would have orgasmed, letting his release loose within his trousers, but the voice compelled him to wait just a little longer.

Once his prey was deep in the bowels of the alley, Michael appeared. He waited until the meatsack walked past him, then rose up from behind a pile of empty crates. Casually, he approached it, an air of carelessness and superiority about him, his height seeming to grow with each step until he towered above his prey.

Suddenly he struck outward, grabbing it by the neck with just one hand. Squeezing, he angled its neck at that most perfect of angles and grinned wickedly. A large vein pulsed there, the bloodrush singing sweetly to Michael from under the meatsack's skin. Michael could feel its heart beating fast, near to bursting from the intensity of the erotic images and phantom caresses he projected into its mind.

As he listened to the blood flowing within it, Michael felt the changes that came only with the growing hunger. His teeth elongated into sharp daggers—their true natural state—and it felt wonderful to let them come out to play. Leaning forward, he inhaled the heady scent of fear and arousal emanating from his prey. It shuddered, overwhelmed by the continuous stream of carnal imagery in its mind's eye. It gazed at him, pleading for sexual and physical release.

It was time.

Dragging its neck close, Michael leaned forward, closing his eyes as he slanted his mouth over the man's neck, and bit down. Teeth sank into salty flesh, the blood still tart and sweet from drink as it flowed warmly over his tongue. Vitality fled the meatsack traitorously while it moaned, and to Michael it sounded lustful, not unlike a very, *very* satisfied lover. He felt the power, the gratification, the heat all flowing into him, and it was a dark kind of heaven—a silken and seductive bliss. With such rich contentment, Michael didn't care that his prey was dying, its essence draining away right there in his very arms. He welcomed the strength that washed over him, the rush of energy and excitement that surged within his body.

Without warning, his food gripped the arm that wrapped around its chest and kept it suspended. The ferocity of its grip startled him, and he paused to look into its eyes again. This time he saw stark fear, sheer terror, and pain. Its eyes were begging Michael to stop, and he could feel the lingering of his own humanity clawing him to pieces inside. Yet, instead of letting go, he resumed feeding. He was feverish now, clutching and grasping so fervently that he almost broke his prey in half. He drank as if he could taste its soul, infused with thoughts that he could possibly claim it for himself. Ideas swam in his mind: it was a kind of hope that he could still get rid of this curse—this damned existence. Desperation made him practically rip the man open in his lust for a surrogate soul.

But there was no salvation to be found. No soul, no cure, no resolution. What was once a man fell to the ground, limp, pale, and lifeless. Michael watched the body, wondering if he would see the moment the soul left it behind, but it never happened. Covered in blood, snow settled softly on its large coat, blanketing him in a shroud of variegated pink. Silence crept back into the cold, dank alleyway.

Realization came over him. As surely as he knew it to be winter, Michael knew he was more than a monster—he was a murderer. There was no good deed that could ever redeem him. He was beyond broken, and there wasn't anything that could fix him. If he thought he could have died from it, he would have torn out his own heart in that moment, but it was no longer possible. Instead, he stood in the darkness, agonizing over a corpse he had created, and wanting to scream out the steam held within his lungs. Overwhelmed with feelings he couldn't even identify, he turned and ran.

He ran right into *her*.

"So, you finally did it. Good! Very good. I was wondering when you would finally feed, Michael." Standing in the lamplight at the alley entrance, the hood of her emerald cloak cast her face in darkness, but her voice was the same. He had never forgotten it. Her eyes were small, spring green fires flickering in the hood's shadow. Long ago, he had thought her eyes were lovely. Now he realized they were cold...calculating... Now he knew looks were indeed deceiving.

Stumbling backward, he fell and lost his balance, landing on top of the body. He quickly scrambled to his feet, glaring at her and wiping the bloody snow from his pants. Stiffening as she approached, he swiftly stepped aside as she moved past him. Unfortunately, he flinched when she grazed his hand at his side, and he chastised himself for it. Turning around, he watched her kneel down beside the body. *The body.* It hurt him to think it had been a man moments ago. As she slipped a cream-colored glove from her right hand, he watched her reach out and dip a pinky finger into the wound he had made. Bringing it back to her lips, her fingertip painted in blood, she sucked on it tenderly.

Turning to Michael, her finger still in her mouth, she purred. "Mmm, that was a tasty one. Do I detect brandy? Perhaps wine?" At his pained, resentful expression, she smiled and stood. Pushing back her hood, she sauntered toward him. Too vain to care about standards, she wore no wig; she wouldn't dare cover up such naturally beautiful hair. Her long, strawberry blonde curls were piled high this evening atop her head, with several soft tendrils framing her face and grazing her collarbone. Her face had been powdered white but her cheeks were rosy, belying the fact that no life existed in her frame. Pouting her tart pink lips, she said, "Aww, you are upset. Come here, my dear."

She opened her arms to him, and he took a step back on instinct. She froze, momentarily taken aback, but it quickly passed. Bringing her arms back down, she folded them across her chest.

"You think I would hurt you?" she inquired. With her brightest smile, she added, "That is very wise, darling. Very wise indeed." She tilted her head and looked him over. "You look to be in serious need of a wash. Where *have* you been sleeping, Michael?" Disdain dripped heavily from her silver-forked tongue.

Michael stood his ground. "My business is no concern of yours, demon. Why are you here?"

She arched a golden eyebrow. "No concern? Why, dearest...I *made* you. You would have no business if not for me." She took a step toward him. "I came to check on your progress."

"My progress?"

"Mmm, yes. Nothing you do is without my knowledge." She smirked, her angelic face turning devilish for a moment. "It seems you have made very significant steps forward. Yet, I do realize you still have much to learn."

"There is nothing you could possibly teach me."

"Au contraire, mon amour. I do find my bed to be very cold of late..." A sly smile adorned her features. "I demand your company, Michael. Join me this evening."

He couldn't hide the shock from his voice. "You want me to join you...? In bed?"

"Of course, silly boy."

"You're, you're mad!"

She threw her head back and laughed. "Perhaps. Hmm. Maybe I *am* mad to seek you out," she mused. "Then again, perhaps I simply discovered I have a preference for your company in particular." She began moving again, slinking closer. "Regardless, I want you as my companion."

"Stop right there," growled Michael, and she did, in fact, pause. "A companion? What kind of 'companion' could I possibly be for you?" What had started as fear of her gave way to simmering anger. "Oh no, *dear*. You could not possibly want a street rat like me. You and I both know you rid yourself of me months ago with your lies."

She frowned. "I never li—"

"You lie now! Be gone, evil temptress! I want none of you or your ilk."

"My ilk?" she sputtered before chuckling. "How humorous..."

She came closer still, radiating desire and wantonness with each step. She was a poisonous, seductive snake, slithering sensually until it was the right time to strike. "I know you make an excellent lover, Michael: we *have* had our dalliances, haven't we? But no, that's not the only reason I chose you. I know your mind offers more. My...*ilk*, as you call them, agree you would be a welcome partner in my endeavors—*all* of my endeavors."

Her ability to entice and persuade always assisted her with a challenge; however, Michael's anger was something she hadn't expected. Pausing, she angled her head to better contemplate his fuming countenance. Despite his urchin-like state, he was still brimming with a regal masculinity and primal strength. "It is *incredibly* fascinating," she murmured. "I seem to find myself more attracted to you every time I see you. Perhaps you have bewitched me? Or corrupted my intentions?" After a moment of quietly perusing him with her eyes, she shook her head. "Regardless, you *are* coming back with me, and I will have you as my companion."

Feeling madness pooling within him, Michael snapped, "No. I have been rid of you, and it will stay that way. Leave me be, witch!"

"Oh, come now, Michael," she said softly and tried to stroke his arm. In a flash, he grabbed her wrist. Her attempt at arousal was like adding fuel to a fire; it only served to enrage him further.

"You came after me, all plots and schemes, and you expect me to believe that you want a partner? Someone to, to, to what? Accompany you through society?" he snapped at her. He clenched his fist, squeezing her wrist tightly as he held it firmly in his grasp. "I know you better than that, *darling*. You don't need me, nor do you consider me your equal. If anything, I would be fodder for your goddamned bedchamber."

The corner of her mouth tilted up. "With everything I have? Honestly... You know, I originally agreed that it could be beneficial to have you by my side as a partner; we could do *magical* things together..." She sighed. "But in hindsight, what else could I possibly need with you?" Her derision was painstaking. "Actually, now that I'm here, I realize I'd much prefer to use you strictly for...physical purposes."

Michael flung her hand away. "You haven't any right to me, maker or no."

She glanced down and saw his hands balling into fists, his white knuckles bright against the darkness. Feigning ignorance, she sorrowfully asked, "Come now, whatever is the matter?"

Michael snarled, furious at her words. "Whatever is the matter? WHATEVER IS THE MATTER? My life, my family, my entire *world*—all of it was destroyed by you! I have nothing left—*nothing*. You reduced my entire being into mere shreds of my former self, just so you could have a damned playmate!" Feeling his sanity abandoning him, he struggled to get the words out, to get her to understand what he knew she had done to him. "You... You... Fuck! By all that is holy, don't you see? You made me into a monster!"

She sighed, as if dealing with a petulant child and turned away. "Really now... We spoke about all of this months ago. You *know* I was forced to dispose of your family." Glancing backwards, a single, lustrous ringlet slid over her pale shoulder. "Frankly, it's ridiculous that you're still this despondent over it."

"They were my family, you she-devil! I don't care if my father found out about your business plans. We both know he wouldn't have said anything to the Governor. He was honorable. Lord help me, if you had simply *talked* to the man!"

She turned to face him, a mere dozen feet away. All he wanted to do was to wrench out her eyes—through her throat. As they gazed at each other, she opted for her usual tactic: she lied, with sweetness in her smile and sugar on her tongue.

"I did talk to him." Michael's eyes widened before her. "He was set on speaking to the Governor, so I did what I had to do. And in the middle of it all, you walked in... C'est la vie." She gestured casually with her hand, as if she had been caught chastising the servants.

Suddenly she was a foot to his left, her movement a mere blur, softly touching his face. He stiffened at the cold of her fingers, refusing to make eye contact with her. "I had seen you at the docks on previous occasions, and I knew you would make an excellent pet." She dropped her hand and began circling him lazily, like a hawk closing in on its prey, her dress rustling softly. "Indeed, I came to your family's home looking for *you*, but I thought I might as well handle all of my urgent business. Oh Michael..." she said, exhaling his name. "That night, even in the face of death you were fearless: so alive and youthful, so handsome... I knew if I could just make you mine..." She sighed, pausing for a moment in remembrance. But her sweetness faded when she saw his anger rising, his nostrils flaring.

She glared at him, her eyes burning with hostile intent. "I gave you a choice, boy. Either you could die by my hand, or you could continue on, carrying on your father's name." With every word, her voice grew louder and more ominous. "I vowed to help you and show you what life could offer. I told you we could live free, with no boundaries or laws, and that you could be more powerful than your wildest imaginings. I offered you a lasting legacy, and it could have been yours. All of this could have been yours! I promised you eternal riches, and I was true to my word!"

She stopped, realizing her voice had betrayed her in its volume and tone. Regaining her composure, she calmly, quietly said, "*You* chose, Michael. *You* did, and it was done without the slightest hesitation on your part. Or don't you remember?"

Again, her seductive nature took hold, and words coated in honey ushered from her lips once more. "I can help you, darling, to remember? You loved my method of persuasion..." She reached for him, but he roughly shoved her hands aside, causing her to stumble.

"No," he whispered angrily. "You lied to me then, and you're lying to me now. My father was a good man—a man of honor. You never spoke with him, and you never told me that your deception would turn me into this, this 'thing.' You said that I would have a 'new appreciation for life,' but you never, ever told me I would kill to have it." He looked at his feet, his rage so strong his voice was barely audible. "You damned me. You damned me to Hell."

"You and I danced, sweeting. I gave you my kiss, which you eagerly accepted, and we sealed the pact. I told you what you would become, and you begged me for it." Laughing, she turned away from him, adding, "You begged me for it the whole night through."

Michael shook his head and ground out, "You made me into a demon—a night creature—this thing I've become. I...I am a plague on this earth. If I had known—"

"If you had known," she interrupted harshly, "you would not be alive." Her gown swishing as she turned, she pointed a talon-like fingernail in his direction. "If you had known, you would have refused my offer. If you had known, I would have killed you."

She lowered her hand and placed it on her hip. One of her beautiful eyebrows rose up, as did her chin, a haughty air about her now. Casually, she murmured, "I would have done it slowly, of course. There wouldn't have been any recourse to do it otherwise."

"Well," snarled Michael, "now that we have established just how much of a vile, devious bitch you are, what in hell's name do you think would make me crawl back into bed with you?"

Her bright green eyes smoldering, she puckered her tart lips and said, "For old times sake?"

"Not on your evil, wretched life."

Her smile dropped, a look of serious displeasure overtaking her alluring face. "Are you truly refusing me?"

"With every ounce that I am," he angrily assured her. The rage inside of him was digging and biting and clawing to get out.

"Ah, well then," she stated matter-of-factly. "I will have to renounce my original offer." She glanced down, working to remove her other glove. "I will have to kill you this evening, lover. My apologies if you don't want to die, but I am afraid you have truly left me with no alternatives." She parted her rich green velvet skirts and leaned down to her thigh. Sliding a brilliant pewter dagger from her garters, she rose up. Standing there, her tantalizing form still capable of bewitching him, she wound a strand of strawberry gold curl around her index finger. "I must say this grieves me, as much as I am capable of grieving. I do feel that I should tell you how much I will miss the time we spent together."

"Go to hell," whispered Michael, positioning himself low, ready for her to strike.

With a fiendish smile full of razor-sharp white teeth, she lunged for him. Her blade glinted in the moonlight, slicing through the air as if in slow motion. Michael grabbed for it and missed, for where the dagger had been, it no longer was. To that end, where she had been, she, too, no longer was. No, suddenly she was *behind* him, latching onto his shirt, and driving her blade into his back, piercing his left shoulder. He grimaced at the burning pain but didn't dare stop, aware his monstrous form would quickly heal—and she would take advantage of any weakness. He spun around, but she had disappeared yet again. In the darkness, her arrogant laughter softly drifted to him.

"I have been alive longer than you think, boy. I know tricks that you can't begin to comprehend." Her voice lowered to a whisper. "I will take your essence into me and remain long after you have departed."

Visions of death and her tearing his father apart assailed him. She was invading his mind, assaulting him with the memory of his father's death. He gripped his head, willing the images to quiet from his thoughts. Once they stopped, he stood still, listening for her movement.

Suddenly her breath caressed his ear. "I will be sure to think of you from time to time."

As her lips touched him, he was already reaching to his right. He yanked her backward, and she landed on her side, the dagger flying out of her hand into the snow. She looked up just as he attacked, gasping at the impact, and dodging his blows while throwing some of her own using her sharp talons.

Michael grabbed her neck with both hands and squeezed, twisting and wrenching, working desperately to free her head from her slender neck. As he did so, she scratched and tore at him, fighting with every ounce of her strength. Stripping hunks of flesh from his chest and shoulders, she pushed and shoved, making feverish attempts to free herself from his grasp. They wrestled viciously, gouging and slashing each other like wild animals. Rolling violently on the frozen ground, they inflicted injury upon injury to each other.

All of a sudden, she shoved away from him, panting like a wild animal, growling low in her throat. She held her hands like claws, the talons longer than any fingernails he'd ever seen on a woman. He got up, rapidly taking in his surroundings like a seasoned warrior on the battlefield. Fury bled into her eyes but also a kind of panic. In that moment, Michael knew she was realizing she had miscalculated him: she had misjudged what he was capable of.

At almost the same time, they each leapt to the roof, their flights easy because of their nature. Michael landed mere feet from her, crouched low like a beast ready to spring. Abruptly he ran at her; he wanted her to have as little time as possible to think. Her eyes widened and she tried to run, but he brutally slammed into her. As soon as she fell, he took hold of her left leg, jerking her towards him. Grabbing her thrashing frame from the rooftop, he swung her upwards as hard as he could and watched her fly. She hurtled up a couple dozen feet before plummeting back down, landing near him with a shout of pain. He watched as her body, suspended in midair, spasmed and jerked.

The candlemaker's shop beneath them featured one of the new lightning rods that had become so popular. She had landed on it perfectly, as if she had intended to show others just how it should be done. She faced upward on it, her left hand grasping the rod where it rose up out of her torso, her right arm hanging limply by her side. Her milk-white slender calves dangled just so, booted feet grazing the rooftop planks. The green fabric of the cloak draped around her, giving the appearance she was merely a sleeping queen.

Michael descended to the ground swiftly, retrieving her dagger from the powdery drift it was buried in. He looked at the rooftop, contemplating whether to run from her death or bear witness to it. After a moment, when the fight seemed to have left her fully, he climbed up to the roof once more. She rested several feet above him, so he climbed on top of the rod's smaller platform to better reach her.

He was ready to bear witness.

Approaching her still form, Michael was surprised to see her squeeze her eyes closed, her pale face briefly contorting in pain. She sighed and coughed, choking on her blood, her maker's blood, and the blood of all her victims through the ages.

"Just finish this, would you?" she asked, her words soft and weak. Even in death, she had the audacity to sound exasperated. "I do find this rather awkward, darling."

Michael paused, consumed by an emotion he hadn't felt since the moment he died. He had hated her so much, loathed her very being for so long and with everything he had. She was right here in front of him, a lamb for the slaughter. No one needed to know the nightmare she had put him through. No one deserved to be subjected to the agony she could bestow. Now he had the option to kill her, to finish her, to eradicate her from this world.

Yet, in the midst of his fury, he began to feel the light of humanity spill outward. He began to think somehow, *maybe*, he could let her live... Perhaps she could redeem herself? Atone for her depraved and heinous crimes? Maybe there was a chance she could experience deliverance. Maybe she could repent and prevent his retribution...

He began to tell her he would try to help her make amends when she gasped. Her body had begun to slip downward, and she gripped the rod urgently to stop her descent. Holding on firmly, she kept herself in place with every ounce of her remaining strength. The rosiness gone from her cheeks now, her face bore a painful grimace as she struggled to keep from crying out.

Catching his eyes on her, she sacrificed her remaining time to posture and fixed him with an icy stare. "I will not beg, Michael." With the poise of the most noble of women, she turned her attention back to the night sky.

Remembering that a truly dead soul could never find salvation, Michael no longer hesitated. With a pang of human guilt, he stood over her and slammed the blade into her chest, forcing it down into her heart. He buried it up to the hilt, spearing the black organ that lay deep within her chest.

She screamed. The sound was nearly impossible to hear unless you were a monster like her—like *him*. Her body shuddered, wracked with something only she could identify, then burst into bright, blue flame. In the moonlight, it was difficult to see unless you were as close as he was. Michael hadn't known what would happen—it was pure instinct that told him what he needed to do. Seeing her final death, he knew what his own fate would be. Stepping back, he watched as her flesh was destroyed, her form disintegrating, reducing to nothing but ashes so light they simply blew away on the freezing wind. No longer suspended by her frame, the dagger fell, loudly thudding as it collided with the wooden roof planks.

Michael lingered for a moment, as still and silent as the cold night had become. Stooping down to collect her dagger once more, the wind suddenly kicked across his face. He stroked his finger across the shining blade, then set off across the rooftops of the city.

He had to get out. He didn't care where he was going, who he would meet, or even the lies he would have to tell. He traveled fast and light, only carrying himself and the weapon of her destruction. Soon he was beyond the city, running through the night down a dark road, dirty snow under his feet and farmhouses a blur to his vision. He made his way deep into the woods, feeling bushes and branches scratching at his arms and legs. Wolves howled sweetly to each other and swaying trees groaned in the moonlight. The brisk clean air of night filled his lungs, and he saw the future stretched out before him.

Still, he kept running.

All he cared about, all he knew, was that he would never, *ever* be like her. He had almost succumbed to the darkness, the malevolence that had been her master. It had almost become his. But there had been a spark of humanity buried inside of him. A small touch of light that brought him back. He had taken a man's life tonight, and while he was unable to give it back, he would never forget what had come from that man's gift.

Michael swore an oath to himself as he ran, an oath to his dead family and for the future. He would not kill or take the life of any human ever again. He would not be a demon. He would not be a monster. He would cease the life she had created for him and begin a new one. He would find happiness and purpose.

As he ran, Michael thought of the years ahead of him and how many would be alone, with no one by his side. *She* had promised him false love, all those years ago when she seduced him. *She* convinced him the only person that would ever love him was her. Now she was gone. He realized that was also a lie, and it gave him hope.

Someday, somehow, he would find love again.

He ran on into the night, hoping one day it may actually be his truth.

Chapter One

The Beginning of Everything

I, Cecelia Moore, was truly and utterly surrounded. Without a doubt, I was trapped while the movie-like scene played out around me. I stood in the middle of a circle of men, swathed in black from head to toe. These were corrupt, ruthless thugs, and they worked for *Him*. Doves flew out of the chapel at their backs, crossing between He and I while we aimed high-caliber weaponry at each other.

I couldn't recall how I got here. It all felt so familiar, though. He was in the shadows, His face hidden by a mask, long white hair spilling out from behind His head in a neat ponytail. Rich green eyes bore into me from within the mask, and I felt a burning in my chest as if I was being pierced by His gaze. I held my ground, reaffirming my stance on the grass, pushing back at His stare by focusing my aim. My booted feet dug securely into the ground, and my confidence was solid.

"One in the head, two in the heart," I muttered to myself and pressed my lips together tightly.

At the edge of the grounds sat an assassin, dressed like a slick Mexican guitarist, casually playing melancholy music. Despite his still form, there was something a bit dramatic about him. He took in the action from the sidelines, simply a mercenary—an assassin—with no personal ties to anyone or anything but himself. The sun's reflection was blinding, stinging my eyes from where it bounced off his dark sunglasses.

Why was he also familiar?

I knew the local and federal authorities as well as international spy agencies were all closing in, mere minutes away. The deadline was drawing to a close, and if I didn't get that vial of antidote from Him in time, my sister would die. She would suffer horribly before her body would unleash a deadly virus into the Los Angeles population, and millions of people would be killed.

But then I realized that He wasn't just anyone—it was a famous B-movie actor. For that matter, the Spanish assassin wasn't who he appeared to be either: he was a crush from high school that I hadn't seen in years. Just like then, he remained a pale version of a sexy Spanish movie star, only with bright, icy blue eyes.

Suddenly I couldn't walk and fell down in the grass. No one paid any attention, and I crawled away, wanting to get out of there before the guns they were both carrying began to sing. The doves started alighting on my shoulders, and I couldn't get them to leave me alone. Then the assassin stood up across the grassy field, his guitar case opening to reveal his own array of guns. He aimed a dark handgun at a dove perched on my right shoulder.

From far away, I heard a woman's voice calling out to me: "Celie! Celie, babe—have you seen my keys?"

I flinched and woke up, rolling over and tangling into my blanket as I fell off the couch. That is, the couch that I had totally forgotten I was sleeping on.

"Ow," I grumbled, glad I hadn't hit the coffee table on the way to the floor. I looked up and saw Kat watching me with a perfectly groomed eyebrow arched in amusement.

"Nice trip," she said. One hand was on her hip, the other hung at her side clutching a new, black Coach purse. All ready to go, she was stylishly dressed, done up in a black pinstripe skirt and red button-down silk blouse. Her short, sunny blonde hair was straight and slicked back to showcase her gorgeous bone-structure. White gold hoops glistened at her delicate ears, and a simple white gold chain lay around her slender neck. I glanced at her feet and saw she had strappy, skinny black heels on. Her toes were perfectly manicured.

Like I said—stylishly dressed as always.

"Yeah, I wish you could've been there," I said tersely. I really did hate waking up like that. "What was it that you needed?" I asked, rubbing the sleep from my eyes. "I thought you asked for something...?"

"Yeah, my keys," she said, frowning. "I've looked everywhere for them and can't find them. Have you seen them around?" Her brow furrowed, her light green eyes troubled. "If I don't find them soon, I'm going to be late for my interview." She set her purse down on the couch and started rummaging through it. "Why do I lose things all the damn time? I mean seriously—what the hell?"

"Can't help ya, man. The last time I saw them, they were in your hand, and you were going to the bathroom to fix your makeup," I said.

Kat shot straight up. "Damn it—that's right! I left them on the counter in there. Jesus—I am so out of it!" she called over her shoulder as she marched to the bathroom. After a few seconds, she came out jingling her keys and winked at me. "'Preciate it, dude. See you later!"

"Alright. Let me know how it goes!" I shouted at the door as it shut behind her.

I crawled back onto the couch and sat wrapped up in my soft, sea green throw, my long auburn hair draped around me. Closing my eyes, I inhaled the lingering scent of the dragon's blood incense I had lit hours ago. I didn't know exactly how to meditate, but I had the gist of it and thought I would give it a shot. After some deep breathing, I tried to feel the energy of the earth flowing into my root chakra and my stress flowing up and out of my crown chakra. Breathe in, breathe out. Breathe in, breathe out. I did this for 5 or 10 minutes, waiting for my normal daily anxieties to leave me and for calmness to come flooding in. Eventually, the only thing that had left me was the feeling in my left foot. I wound up stomping around the living room, trying to get my foot to wake up while looking like a dancing Neanderthal.

What was going on? For almost three whole weeks, I was having these weird, off-the-wall dreams about guns and bad guys and doves. Most of them involved the same assassin guy, but I could never remember his name. Jay? Robin? Hawk? It was something with a bird in it. The guy showed up in almost every dream, always looking like a guy from my past, but I still *knew* it was him. After a while, I couldn't sleep in my bed because my dreams were even more intense there. My appetite was reduced to nothing, and my enthusiasm for normal fun things was basically non-existent. I had been crawling out to this couch every night, sometimes sleepwalking to it, and I still didn't have any answers. Nothing was improving.

Better yet, did I mention that I had no idea who this guy was? No matter who he managed to look like, it was never anyone I had seen recently. They were all from at least ten years ago, if not longer. Plus, in all the years I had been living in this city, I had never met anyone with a bird-like name. The whole thing felt absurd. *I* felt absurd. It was as if whoever that was in my dream was hiding from me, letting me get glimpses of him from time to time.

Honestly, this was how things had always been. My life had been perpetually filled with Ripley-style items of the weird and freakish. Since I was young, I had always been a little bit psychic. Pretty regularly, I had dreams about events that would happen, and I would get a little weirded out. I knew about a going-away party before it happened. I would regularly ask for things as people were coming home—things they had just purchased. I regularly had déjà vu, too.

Even more freakish were my ghost encounters. When I was eight years old, I encountered ghosts knocking things over, but one night one came to visit me in my room. My mother never believed me about it, as if it was preferable for me to have had a vivid and gut-wrenching nightmare. However, I remember it clear as day, even now: how the ghost had turned its head to look at me, extending its arm to point in my direction before stepping down off my vanity toward me. It was incredibly creepy. I never saw it again, but a month or two later, a long wood-frame picture fell off the wall right next to my head. Nothing had touched it, and it had been hanging there for years. I would get phone calls from the dead sometimes, too, but that was usually my grandmother.

Then there are instinctual vibes I get about certain people. That's an entirely separate story...

After spending a solid thirty minutes trying to stomp the feeling back into my foot, I gave up the idea that I could make my life stress-free and decided I needed to get ready for work. I dragged myself up the stairs into the shower. Once I was done and my hair was blown dry, I threw on normal 'business casual' attire: black dress pants, a white blouse, and a black cardigan. I grabbed my favorite griffin pendant necklace and some small silver hoops. My grandmother's charm bracelet was the finishing touch. Having her with me always left me feeling like I was complete. Maybe that's because she was more of a mother to me than any I could have wished for. Putting on low black heels, I grabbed my keys and purse, then headed out the door for the office.

Trudie Meyers was already there; I was sure of it. Her bleach-blonde, athletic, and heavily caffeinated soccer mom style always made me cringe as soon as I walked in the front door. I could hear her Georgia accent, sweetness dripping off her tongue as she spouted lie after lie, cozying up with every customer who walked in the door, and leaving me feeling like I needed to rip off my own head. I could handle fake people about as well as the next person, but someone who was that pretentious and duplicitous? No, thank you. Trudie was a two-faced perfectionist, eager to ingratiate herself in other people's business and to make herself the hero of any negative situation. As soon as they left the room, she was quick to gossip about them. She was also quick to look down on anyone who didn't have as much money as her—and to want the business of anyone who had more.

Every fiber of my being wanted to throttle her. Whenever I was greeted with her tanned, lithe frame, cold blue eyes, and Macy's womenswear, all I saw was someone I loathed. I would never be like her, and I think it annoyed her that I didn't want to be.

Barbieri Insurance had been my employer for two years, and it was a pure struggle. If I didn't need to pay my bills, I would have found something more agreeable to my creative side. Maybe a coffee shop? But this was it for the moment, and every day was hell. Public scrutiny, cliques with the other staff, and critiquing of every facet of the job. Her husband would stop by sometimes, talking about his fascination with the newest weight-loss program and how they could spend their money after acquiring other insurance offices. Their children, who sometimes helped out at the office, were gifted with brand new cars, big vacations out of the country, and anything they could possibly want without fear of having to live up to any expectations or take on any responsibilities. It was publicly thrown in everyone's face, every day, that we were the help. Despite the lavish lifestyle they lived, and the hard work and care we provided to their customers, we weren't important enough to have health insurance or make more than minimum wage. It was the worst business I had ever been a part of and convinced me I would never work in insurance ever again.

But here I was—in the parking lot, sitting in my car. Angry metal music blasted from my radio. I was steeling myself against what I knew would be an onslaught of Trudie because I was five minutes late.

As soon as I opened the door to the office, I began my plan of attack, a way to get through the day and make it out in one piece. Oddly, I reached my desk without incident. Hopeful, I sat down and began booting up my computer.

"Where's Trudie?" I asked Ronnie, our most junior associate. Her long, stick-straight brown hair swung over her shoulder as she turned to answer me.

"Oh, she's out today."

"Out?"

"Yeah. Something with one of the kids."

Of course it was, I thought. "Okay then. Thanks."

I was thankful for the small favor of not having to deal with Trudie today. A second later, I realized the implications. "Wait—who's locking up?"

Ronnie smiled slyly at me. "That would be you."

"Figures," I said. "No offense."

"Well, I opened the office. Makes sense for you to close it."

I shrugged in defeat. "What about Cathy? Where's she at?" Cathy was our other associate who sold life insurance. She was regularly in and out of the office, but that was okay. She was like Trudie's mini-me, dressing like her and acting like her, coloring her hair like her, and following her like a cultist follows the cult leader.

I couldn't stand her either.

Ronnie grinned. "She's out at a client's house trying to get some new policies on the books." Ronnie didn't like Cathy either.

About eight hours and 13 policyholders later, I was done. I had enough paperwork to keep me busy for another hour, so I told Ronnie to pack up and go home. When she left, I locked up the door behind her and returned to my desk, ready to dive in. I didn't have to worry about Cathy showing up and knew I had the office all to myself. The phones and neon sign were turned off, and I had some quiet music going. I bent my head down and began poring over applications for coverage, loss reports, and driving records. In fact, I was at it for about forty minutes before a knock at the door startled me.

The front of the office was all glass, but each window had a bamboo shade that was drawn down over it. The front door was the same, but it clearly had the office hours on it, including an after-hours emergency phone number for reporting accidents and the like. Everything was off, including the lights. There was a small glow from the tiny lamp tucked away in the corner of the main office space, but a wall was in front of it, blocking any visible light from peeking around the shades.

I had no idea who would be trying to come into the office this late at night, and likewise, I had no intention of opening the door, either. A single girl can never be too careful these days, so I was tempted to call the police. However, the strangest urge compelled me to see who it was, so I peeked from around the right side of the door shade.

A man stood outside.

Wait—that's not good enough. He was a *man*, emphasis on the "man" part. Not a boy or a guy, but a tall, perfectly proportioned MAN. He looked to be at least six foot four, broad shoulders under the jacket of his suit, his stance casual, and perhaps my age? He couldn't have been older than his late thirties. His straight, long hair was the color of fresh coffee, and it was pulled back in a ponytail secured with a strand of leather. His eyes were bright grey, like silver, and his face was both strong and soft in all the right places. I stared with my mouth watering at this incredible specimen of masculinity, feeling immensely insecure and aroused all at the same time.

When he looked right at me, I promptly freaked out.

I went batty and squashed the shade tightly to the window. I stood there—motionless—willing myself to become invisible but also wanting to peel back the shade and stare at him again. Ashamed of myself and overwhelmed by the devastating hotness on the other side of the glass, I kept mumbling to myself, over and over again. "Oh my god, oh my god, oh my god, oh my god..." My heart was pounding in my ears, my stomach performing acrobatics in my torso like an amateur. I thought I felt it fall to the floor and slither away in shame at one point.

After a minute, I peeled back the shade, just a centimeter, and silver eyes gazed into mine. I squeaked and shoved the shade back into place. He commenced knocking again, this time sounding persistent. It was the urgency that made me feel obligated to find out what was going on. I stood to the left of the door and, without pulling back any shades, called out to him.

"Hi! We're closed. Our after-hours number is on the door. Unless you need help? I can call the police if you need them...?" The knocking stopped instantly. Then he set out to give me a heart attack by actually responding to me.

"Hey. Um, I need to speak with you." His voice was low, deep, rich, and completely set me on fire. I knew there was potential that I could spontaneously combust around this man. Having him come in was not the best idea. "Is there any chance that I could come in?" A second passed and he added, "Or you could come out here?"

I reasoned with myself that if he was a serial killer, the first mistake I could make would be to continue this conversation. Yet another part of me irrationally reasoned that I would potentially die happy. I did the next best thing that came to mind.

"Sorry, mister, but I'm just the cleaning person! I'm just here to clean...things... You know, like the floor? And dusting. I'm great at dusting. You'll have to come back tomorrow when it's open." I slapped my hand to my forehead and groaned. I knew I sounded like an idiot. I hoped he would believe me. I really did.

But he didn't.

He laughed at me.

Then he called me by my name.

"You're definitely not the cleaning person, Celie. Seriously, this is important. I need you to open the door."

I stumbled backward, partly in shock and partly dizzy. He knew my name! How did this ridiculously attractive man know MY name?! I was no one: I was neither infamous nor invisible. I had no movie credits to my name, no books written by me or about me. I didn't even have any social media accounts for God's sake!

Was it getting hot in here? I jerked when I realized I had stopped breathing. Where did the air go? I felt like I was suffocating. Feeling faint, I leaned forward and put my hands on my knees. I closed my eyes and called to him again, this time with no pretense in my voice.

"Listen, I'm sure you're a nice guy. You seem like a really nice guy—just a nice, nice guy... A handsome guy... A big-shouldered guy..." I had started rambling, trying to steady myself and talk at the same time. It wasn't that easy. I worked up my voice again. "I'm going to be nice back, okay? *Please* go away. Stop banging on the door and leave. I don't want to have to call the cop, but I absolutely will."

I hoped he would listen. I was still leaning forward and put a hand out to push away from the door. I glanced up and saw the dark shadow where he had put his own hand on the other side. I heard him sigh, and somehow, it seemed to set me at ease. I couldn't figure out why, but it did.

"You *really* aren't going to make this easy, are you?" His voice was calm and a smidge exasperated. "Celie, I'm here to help you. That's a good thing—a *non-criminal* thing. I'm not going to hurt you, I swear. Just open the damn door, would you?" A moment later, he added, "*Please.*"

I stared at the door.

"You *know me*, Celie."

Bizarre as it sounded, something about him was familiar. Again, a nagging feeling somewhere in my gut said he was okay. While thoughts of spontaneous combustion into a ball of sex fire made me swoon—and riddled me with nervousness—something about this strange man also left me believing in him. I was weighing his tone, his words, his meaning, and I was considering *trusting* him.

Then a tickling sensation started in the back of my brain. His voice, and the fact that he knew my name, triggered a new thought in my head. All of a sudden, I had something I needed to ask him. It was simple, but before I could let him in, I needed to know.

"Okay. I'll let you in, but only if you answer something first." I stood up and stared at his shadow.

"What's that?" he asked.

I leaned on the door, my hand on the lock and closed my eyes. "Who are you?"

I felt the heat of him through the door, and it was delicious. I was ninety-nine percent sure I knew what he would say, chanting to myself, *'Please be him, please be him, please be him, pleasepleasepleasepleasepleasepleasepleaseplease...'* It was like a mantra to keep me in reality because this felt like a dream.

A dream that was all too familiar.

"You know exactly who I am."

I grabbed the door handle, swung the lock, and opened the door to meet his brilliant pair of silver eyes.

"I'm Michael. Michael Hawkins. And I don't have any guitar case today," he said with a laugh.

That was when I fainted, and boy, did that hurt.

I woke up in his car, which was moving at reasonably fast speeds down the highway. Orange streetlights flashed overhead as he drove, making me wince at the visual stimulation. It was clearly dark out, but I had no concept of time. How long had I been out? My head was throbbing like I was hungover at a rave. The black interior of the speeding car—was it a sports car?—was so dark, I could barely make out my kidnapper at the helm.

A bit scared at being alone, especially with this incredibly hot stranger, I was also really angry. Who the hell did he think he was? You can't just kidnap people, carting them off like a tenth-century Viking. This was reality, and kidnapping meant police, and sometimes even *more* police—and lots of jail time. He must have some big brass balls to nab me from the office in broad daylight. I let him know how angry I was. I sat upright and started punching his right arm.

"What the hell, man? Are you mental?" I shouted in between punches. "You can't just go dragging people off into the night! Someone probably saw you, and you're gonna be in for a world of hurt, friend—a *world* of hurt! The police are going to come after you, and it'll be all over for you and your fast and fancy cars! Yes, sir! That's right—no more suits or expensive—" Gesticulating wildly, I tried to think of *any* word to represent rich people's possessions, but only came up with— "things like this! Yeah! You're gonna go to jail, buddy!"

He didn't do anything. This man—Michael...something?—had no reaction: no flinching, no grimacing, *nothing*. He wasn't paying a single bit of attention to me.

"Damn it, you pain-in-the-ass! Stop this car! Pull over, and let me out! NOW!" I was being as obnoxious and loud as I could be. I was willing to do anything to save myself.

He frowned at me, then turned his attention back to the road, resuming his ignorance of me like a consummate professional.

I huffed and crossed my arms. "You're a rude guy. Anyone ever tell you that? Seriously the rudest man I've ever met. I officially take back any statement I made about you being nice." Sulking, I turned and looked out the passenger window. I figured if he wasn't going to talk to me, I could at least try to figure out where I was and create some kind of escape route. I began playing with the door handle to test it. It was immediately locked from the other side. I tested the window, and he locked that, too.

"I just wanted some air," I mumbled, and shortly after, the A/C vents began to blow soft, cool air across my exposed skin. "Thanks," I muttered.

Nothing looked familiar to me. Not his car, not the passing countryside—nothing. The latter especially worried me. I'd been living here for 20 years and thought I knew most of the area, but I didn't recognize anything that I could make out in the streetlights. It was pure black woods, with an occasional dim light deep in the forest. I could only surmise that we were beyond the city limits and deep into the backwoods. My anxiety was kicking in, and I unconsciously began playing with my grandmother's charm bracelet.

He reached out a hand and gently placed it over mine. I flinched at the contact. His hand was warm and rough, clearly *not* the hand of a businessman. That was another concern: he was in a suit, so if he wasn't a businessman, what was he?

I jumped when he spoke, forgetting just how deep his voice was.

"I'm sorry I didn't wait for you to wake up to leave the city. I didn't have a choice in the matter."

I glanced at him, and he gave me a quick look of apology. I waited for him to keep talking, but he didn't. "So what—you just randomly drag girls off in your car?" I asked.

"No."

A random thought intervened. "Wait a minute there, buddy. You're not some kind of professional, are you? Like a trafficker or something? Have I seen you on some news show or premium channel predator special? Is that why you look familiar?"

"I look familiar?"

"Don't change the subject. Are you going to sell me on the black market? I mean, I'm sure you'd get top dollar, but I really don't want to get chained to some Middle Eastern version of a mafia don."

"No, I'm not some kind of trafficker, and I'm sure as hell not going to bargain you off to a crime lord or Saudi prince." He glanced at me. "Just a hunch, but I'm guessing I wouldn't have you in the front seat if I was." When I huffed, he added, "Just relax, Celie. Everything is going to be fine."

"But that's just it. I can't relax. You're a total stranger *who knows my name*. I'm a little creeped out, and you're telling me everything is going to be fine."

"I told you already. I'm Michael Hawkins," he stated, giving me a quick glance, like that should make all the sense in the world.

"Nope. No clue who you are," I quipped. He groaned. "Listen, I said you're familiar, and you are, but I honestly have no idea where I've seen you before. None."

"You don't remember?"

"Remember what?"

He groaned again. "I'll tell you when we get where we're going."

"Tell me now."

He clamped his mouth shut. I waited, but he refused to continue our conversation. This time I groaned and went back to sulking in my seat.

About a mile down the road, he flipped off his headlights. We drove on for another half a mile, with me panicking silently in the passenger seat. He turned onto a dirt road, and the banjo theme from that redneck Burt Reynolds movie popped into my head. We continued in utter darkness for a few more miles. The woods lining the road were dense, barely illuminated by the moonlight. The night seemed like it was closing in on me, and I was wondering if it would swallow me whole. I realized that the further we drove away from the road, the less likely I could be found if I was hurt, starving, or in need of emergency resuscitation.

Just when I started thinking I really was going to be killed and left for dead, a house came into view. At first glance, it looked like a heap of stone, but drawing closer, you could tell that it was nowhere near that at all—this was a Tudor castle. I could make out a stone turret on the far-left corner toward the back. Small windows decked each floor about ten feet apart, with arches and stained-glass ovals for decoration. The roof was lined with battlements just begging to be walked on for a wonderful view. There was no moat, but there was a garden maze to the left of the building, creating a natural bit of defense around the property. Tall trees lined the drive leading up to the gate. I was dumbstruck by his home.

I let out a soft, breathless 'ooh' before I could catch myself. "This is yours?" I breathed, not taking my eyes from the house.

Michael chuckled. "Yeah, this is mine. You'll see it in just a minute." He pulled up to the gate, which was actually two huge wooden doors held in place by stone columns topped with angry gargoyles. The doors were roughly 15 feet high and probably six inches thick. A keypad was hidden in the bushes just to the left, and Michael reached out his window to enter a series of letters and numbers. The Kong-sized doors opened, and he pulled through, circling around the oyster shell driveway. A waterfall fountain, lush with ferns and backed by several birch trees, took up residence in the center of the circle. A small pond at the base was decorated with happily swimming bright orange koi fish.

Michael stopped just in front of the steps leading to the main house. I began to unbuckle, eager to get out of his car and see this magical place. Putting his car in park, he reached out and put a hand on mine. I looked up, and he was just staring at me.

"Um... Are you going to tell me what's going on now?" I asked quietly. He gave a smile, and my heart skipped a beat—literally. As he climbed out of his car, I quickly followed him out and up the front steps to the main door. He unlocked it and opened it for me. Just inside, he switched on a soft Tiffany lamp that sat on a half-round table in the hall.

Once I entered, I couldn't move. All I could do was stare at the dark woods, the golden walls, and the pristine condition of all the obvious antiques and artwork. A full suit of armor stood by the base of the ornate hardwood stairs. A tapestry of the Knights Templar hung over the door leading to the room on our left. I think he actually was forced to drag me to the right into a sitting room; I wouldn't have budged otherwise.

I followed Michael's direction and sat down on a cozy, moss green sofa. He strode over to a bar in the far back corner. Pouring us both Irish whiskeys, he walked over and set mine down on a stone coffee table in front of us. He sat down in a plush, wingback leather chair just to my left, swallowed a large sip of whiskey, and then began to explain a few things.

"You're not who you think you are, Celie."

Chapter Two

Hiding in the Background

"Not who I think I am? What does that even mean?"

"You're someone very, very important—for all the right and wrong reasons." He paused at my expression. I'm sure it looked like I wanted to laugh. I tended to do that in very serious conversations, and I always had a horrible penchant for displaying my thoughts on my face for the whole world to see.

I could never have been a poker player—or a politician.

"Ah," he said, "You think this is a joke, right? A prank? Something a friend worked up to embarrass you? Sorry, but it's not. No one is videotaping this for posting on social media." I stopped smiling. "I'm one hundred percent serious. I started trying to introduce myself to you probably three or four weeks ago."

I gasped. "The dreams?"

"Yeah, the dreams." He winced and continued. "I didn't think they would bother you like they did. Sorry about that."

I smirked. "Good job." I glanced down at my lap and shook my head before I met his gaze again. "How? I don't understand—how could you have anything to do with my dreams?"

"I'll explain that."

"Good, because I'm really, really confused right now."

"Right." His tone told me to drop it for now. "I'm here because someone is coming for you. They are powerful, and they are dangerous. You need help if you want to fight them."

"Who is this 'someone'?" I asked using air quotes.

"Bad people. Insane people. People that want you with them instead of me. If I don't help you fight, they *will* kill you."

"Wait, wait, *wait*—hold the phone. I'll just go to the police, right? Tell me what you know about them; I'll go to the police, and they can put me in hiding, like a witness protection thing or whatever."

"If I thought you could hide from them, I'd tell you to run, but I don't think you can."

"Right..." I eyeballed him with serious skepticism. "So what do these scary 'bad people' want from me anyway?" My sarcasm game was strong now because I was realizing my handsome stranger was a bonafide crazy person.

What a shame...

Michael cleared his throat, suddenly a bit sheepish. "Well, I know that one of the reasons was because they... Um... How do I put this..." He stood up and walked to the window. He stopped, looked down at his glass and took a final swig from it, tilting his head back to get every last drop. Michael looked back at me, then turned to stare back out at the night. Quietly, he said, "One of the reasons is because they know how much I care about you."

"Whoa," I said, making a 'T' shape with my hands, "Time out. Hold on there, big fella. You don't even *know* me. Other than some weird dreams I've been having—thanks to you, somehow...apparently—you and I are complete and total strangers. Are you sure you're not just confusing me with someone else? Maybe hit your head, got some amnesia, perhaps?" Then my eyes narrowed in suspicion. "Let's talk about how you do that dream thing, actually, 'cause that's some weird shit. I've never heard of anyone doing that kind of thing before. Are you some sort of psy-ops government agent? An experiment run amuck?"

Ignoring me completely, he replied, "I definitely meant to nab you. No amnesia. This is legitimate."

"Then what the hell kind of shit did you get me into?" I exclaimed. I was really confused, one hundred percent freaked out, and feeling like I was going to have some sort of mental breakdown. I took my own glass and downed the whiskey, slamming it back down on the table. Irish whiskey was always my favorite, and it was a good burn.

Michael poured himself another glass before heading back to his chair. He angled it towards me, sat down, and looked right into my eyes. "I saw you about two months ago, coming out of a store on Vineyard Lane. You actually walked past me on the way to your car."

"I think I'd remember you."

"I made sure you didn't."

"How did you—"

"Later. The only thing you need to know is that I literally couldn't take my eyes off of you."

I glanced at the glass on the table. Did I really drink all that whiskey? I felt parched.

Without stopping, he continued. "I'm not sure what it was, but I knew that I wanted to get to know you. I sensed something about you, something I couldn't explain. You were beautiful, and you just looked so innocent... I hadn't seen anyone like you for a long, long time."

Okay—where was that whiskey bottle? My throat was terribly dry—*Sahara Desert dry.*

"I decided to spend a day with you, and I followed you around the city to see what kind of interests you had—"

Again, I made the universal time-out symbol. "So what you're telling me—what I'm hearing you say—is that you were stalking me? That about right?" I queried. My knees were weak, my palms sweaty, my pulse racing: thank God I was sitting down.

Michael sighed. "Well, no, because I wasn't going to hurt you. However, if you're going to be literal about it, then yes, I guess I was stalking you."

"Finally," I replied. "Thanks for being honest with me and admitting it." He appeared half-stunned, half-relieved that I wasn't flipping out. I shrugged. "I still don't know how you did it, but I figured if you can project yourself into my dreams, then you probably could have done a shit-ton worse to me *way* before this."

"Yeah, that..." he said, sounding kind of alarmed that I brought that up again. "I was trying to introduce myself to you, but I didn't know if you would reject me. I thought I would give you a chance to get used to me first."

I could sense his honesty, so it wasn't the 'stalker-lite' activity that had me on edge. My knees were still weak, my throat was still dry, and I was sitting so close to this man that could have killed me but didn't. No, it was his *scent*. This near to him, I was drowning in his intoxicating, rich fragrance. The man smelled like leather and oak and dragon's blood—something masculine and sexy, earthbound and natural.

Moreover, this stupidly attractive man was talking about being drawn to me—ME—'always cute but never beautiful' me. I was the girl who was always the funny friend, the one her other friends brought along to have someone to look better than. My whole life, I was the one who was always left sitting at the table while everyone else was asked to dance. Guys who looked like him never thought of me except to ask if my friends were available.

I had to separate myself from this, from him, just for a moment to bring reality back in. I could not let a handsome face make me become irrational. I stood up and grabbed my glass. His was empty again, and as I reached for it, our fingers touched when he handed it to me. I inhaled sharply but didn't flinch. I turned and walked over to the bar and poured us each some more whiskey.

Bringing it back, I sat down, took a drink, and said, "How did you do it?" Another swig of whiskey and I felt my nerves stop convulsing.

"It's just this thing I learned. Kind of like remote viewing, if you've ever heard of it."

"I've heard of it."

He smiled, and I melted a little inside. I thought I might be here for a while, so I decided to make myself comfortable. I reached down and slipped off my heels. Lifting my legs, I tucked my feet underneath me on the sofa.

"Please, continue," I said and gestured to him.

Clearing his throat again, Michael continued his story. He mentioned places I had gone to, shops I had visited, restaurants I had eaten in... I listened to him describe my day and how he had realized we had much in common. He had asked the bookstore owner what book I was reading and purchased his own copy. He tried some of the food from Garcia's and loved the quesadillas, making sure to have it with a bottle of good cerveza with a shot of top-shelf tequila. He had even purchased some songs from rock and synthwave bands I enjoyed.

We continued talking, and I learned a lot about him. We really did have a lot of things in common, like similar interests and viewpoints. We loved rock music but weren't fans of country. Both of us were drawn to tales of Asgard and Native American culture. Mystical things like tarot cards and palm reading were fascinating, and movies were one of the best ways to pass the time. We also agreed that if more people had a sense of humor these days, the world would have a lot less problems.

Three hours and a bottle of whiskey later, I was lying across his sofa, belly down, watching him in fascination. I couldn't help but ask him, "So why all this secrecy, Hawkins? Why not just come out and ask me on a date or something?" Whiskey always made me bolder, and I could get kind of blunt when I got bold.

"That's another story entirely, Celie," he murmured softly.

"Always with the mysteries! Just tell me. I'm all ears." I smiled at him, the handsome guy who was NOT a serial killer, and realized I was having a blast. How much better could this all get?

Michael took a deep breath, leaning forward in his chair. In this short time, I had carefully watched his movements, observed when certain things were easy for him to talk about, and when others were difficult. I was good at observing people: I'd had years of practice. This time, I knew whatever was coming was hard for him to say.

"Okay. Um, it's like this. I could project my thoughts into the dreams you were having because I have a curse."

"A curse?" I said with a laugh. "Like you-opened-a-tomb-in-Egypt curse? Like a-witch-hexed-you kind of a curse?"

"Something like that."

"Hmm, what other curses are there? Like... Like a werewolf's curse?"

"Not a werewolf."

"But we're getting warm, here?"

"I know some people would say this is all in my head, but I assure you, it's not."

"Okay," I drawled. As he stared at me, his eyes melting me into a tiny puddle of goo, I was completely aware he was dashing my dreams again with some psycho-sounding nonsense.

"I'm a vampire."

Nope. Nope, I did *not* hear that.

"Come again?"

"I'm a vampire."

I stared at him, probably with the blankest of blank looks on my face because I was completely speechless.

"There, I said it." He leaned back, drained his whiskey, and rested his arm on the chair, the glass dangling from his fingers over the side. "I'll sit here while you run away screaming. Totally fine."

I continued to sit there, still as a statue, saying nothing at all. My brain had imploded.

"Any time now..." he muttered.

"Sorry!" I exclaimed, shaking my head. "Sorry, I must not have heard you. You said what now?"

"I. Am. A vampire," he said, leaning into the words for emphasis.

"A *what*?" I asked, because this needed major clarification.

"Here we go," he mumbled to himself. Speaking louder, he began to explain his...*situation*. "Alright, let's start with this: I'll tell you what I'm *not*. I am *not* lying, and I am not trying to deceive you. I am *not* a nut or some escaped mental patient—my sanity is fully intact. I am not on any drugs: prescription, homemade, or otherwise. And I don't see dead people." He paused. "Wait—I take that last one back. But I am telling you the truth."

I couldn't believe what I was hearing. This man in front of me, Michael, was telling me he was a vampire: a blood-sucking, cape-wearing, bat-transformational vampire. He sincerely believed he was this 'creature of the night' business—I could see it on his face—but how could I possibly believe him? Why should I believe him? He was a pretty face, and, in my experience, they all had agendas—games they liked to play. Maybe this was all a ruse, some elaborate diversion to waste his 'more money than god' time.

After a moment of silence on both our parts, all I could manage was two words: "Prove it."

He frowned. Either he didn't expect to have to do that after all of our conversing, or he didn't want to have to go that far. "I am not lying to you about this," he pushed back. "This is not something normal people make up."

"Right," I replied. "Normal people. *Normal.* You sound absolutely batshit—pun *not* intended." He scoffed. "Listen, if you want me to believe it, you're going to have to give me more to work with. Prove it to me. Put your money where your mouth is."

Michael put down his drink and leaned forward. Opening his mouth, I watched as his canines grew, lengthening into sharp points that hung almost a quarter of an inch beyond his other teeth. That boldness given to me by the whiskey kicked in, and I reached out and poked at one of his canines with my index finger, startling him. It seemed real enough, and I sat back on the sofa. He closed his mouth and stayed silent, waiting for me to speak.

In my head, I evaluated our entire conversation: his demeanor, this house, my instincts—everything. Some things didn't fit, though. For one, he drank whiskey. For another, he followed me around in daylight. His home wasn't decked out in an all-black and red goth motif, either. He didn't fit the bill of a standard, Stoker-esque vampire or one of those Twilight sparkly guys. There was no Lost Boy attitude, and he was too attractive to be a Nosferatu-type.. I needed more answers.

"So," I began, "what's this all about? You aren't exactly what I expected a vampire to be like. Are you going to suck me dry? Make me a goth bride? You going to drain me and feed me to the wolves or something? And how did you manage to be outside during the day? Isn't that against the rules or something?"

He looked shocked. Not only was I *not* running away screaming, but I was asking him legitimate questions.

"I— I'm not like they describe in books, if that's what you're asking—"

"Exactly. That's exactly what I'm asking."

"—but I do have some redeeming qualities."

I was still wrapping my head around how he was a vampire. Like him, *I* was even confused about why I wasn't scurrying out of there. "And? What are they?"

"I can go out if I fed the night before," he said, and I made a face like I would puke. "No, no, not that kind of feeding. I only drink blood from—" Again, I made a face that said he needed to find me a bucket. "Argh. I don't drink from *people*, Celie."

"Oh?" I straightened up in my seat. "You don't?"

"No, I get it from a blood bank. They think I need daily transfusions for a rare anemic-like condition. I told them I have a private physician that takes care of me."

"Well, that's new."

"Getting back to my explanation... I had fed the night before, so a day in the sun doesn't bother me, as long as it's limited exposure. Also, I didn't follow you *every* day, just one or two here and there."

"And the whiskey? I thought your type only drank—well, you know..." I scrunched up one side of my face and motioned outward.

"Myth," he said.

"Okay then." I thought for a minute before saying, "I just have one more question."

"Shoot."

"How old are you?" I asked. Playing along with this whole 'vampire' business got my curiosity going. I figured, if he was making this up—if those extremely realistic porcelain veneers were actually the real deal—well, he would probably say he'd been alive for thousands of years. He might say he was from a century when men believed in multiple gods. Maniacs never come up with normal stuff, so it was a safe bet that this would prove he was nuts.

"About two hundred and fifty years old—give or take a decade."

Or not.

"Ah," I murmured, my theory foiled again. "Um, are you sure you don't mean two thousand and fifty? Or twelve hundred and fifty?"

With a puzzled expression, he said, "No. Why?"

"No reason. Just making sure you haven't lost it." I quickly changed the subject. "So these people that want to kill me... You said they were really after you?"

Michael stood up and started pacing across his plush red and gold oriental rugs. Staring at their patterns, I oddly wondered what it would be like to roll around on them naked. I was always one for random thoughts like that—particularly ones that belonged in a gutter. Being around such a sexy man—er, vampire—only gave me impure thoughts of the highest order. It was no wonder I didn't hesitate to think about having a dalliance with him on the beautiful rug at my feet.

All of a sudden, I became aware that he had stopped speaking or moving. I looked up to see why and found him staring at me—*hard*. '*Oh my god, he knows what I'm thinking...*' I felt myself blushing, the heat in my cheeks like flames on the sides of my face, and all he did was smile at me. A very wicked, promising, *knowing* kind of smile.

I cleared my throat in embarrassment. "You were saying?"

He laughed out loud and walked over to the bar. Pouring us each a brandy—always suitable for a nightcap—he handed it to me. Then he surprised me by sitting down next to me, clearly feeling comfortable enough to be near me. Surprising myself, I allowed it.

Honestly, all of this was going so fast! I couldn't have imagined waking up this morning knowing I was going to be this relaxed, this at ease with someone who had kidnapped me to his castle in the woods and told me he was a vampire—after admitting to *stalking* me, to boot! I must've been going out of my mind, but I really had no fear of him at all. I felt like I had known him for such a long, long time. Maybe it was those dreams? Did I have some sort of Stockholm syndrome? All I knew was that I was not about to pass up the chance to sit cozy with a bona fide sex god.

I mean, you tell me where the problem lies in that situation?

"So the bad guys," Michael began, "are actually cult members. They're headed up by a man named Devlin Raines. He's been off the radar for a while, so the authorities don't have him high on their lists anymore. I think most—if not all—of the cases that involved him are cold now."

"What is this cult obsessed with?" I inquired. He stood up and started moving around the room again, lighting candles and small lamps. The glow warmed the room just like the brandy warmed me. "What do they want?"

He paused in his activities. "Me."

"What do you mean?"

"It goes back to the early-eighties, when Devlin was a scientist working for EvRad Chemicals, a corporation dealing in biological engineering."

Just hearing the words 'biological engineering' gave me the chills. Now I understood why he was lighting the room. I had long been a believer that nature was not to be tampered with. Scientists didn't even fully understand the human body, let alone the human brain, but they were always ready to create diseases and weapons of war in an attempt to scare other countries into submission.

"Let me guess. You worked for EvRad, too?"

"No."

"Oh. Well, never mind then."

Michael sat back down, looking at me intently. "Raines was...he was formulating the basic components for biological weapons—deadly gases like VX and the like. His work involved combining a multitude of variations to create the ultimate arsenal for the government."

"To fight the Russians?"

"No. Actually, he—and you'll never believe this—"

"I'm believing a lot these days."

"—he wanted to help *them* fight *us*. He thought our system of government was dissolving, that we were corrupt and destructive—becoming unstable. He wanted us to remember what we had created the United States for in the first place: freedom, independence, democracy. Raines thought we had been abusing these privileges, and he wanted to be the one to deliver our punishment."

I leaned sideways against the back of the sofa and focused on Michael. "Sounds like a sadistic whack job. Did he ever come up with anything? I've never heard of him."

"Luckily, no. A spy within EvRad leaked out what he was doing to the FBI. He was brought in for questioning, and everything they tried to accuse him of, he denied. Without any evidence to support the accusations, they were forced to let him go." At my puzzled look, he added, "All of his research had been split into various locations, so they couldn't piece it all together; they didn't have the resources.

But the damage from the investigation was done. EvRad fired him immediately. In their case, bad press was really bad. Raines left the states and went overseas to France. He found a job with a research organization and continued developing a bio-toxin for the Russians. A few years later, after much trial and error, Raines realized he needed a strain of anthrax to complete his testing, and he attempted to purchase it through an undercover operative. Some agencies had been investigating illegal weapons trafficking with the Russians and heard Raines was working on something for them. U.S. federal authorities worked with international ones already watching his actions. This time, he was arrested and sentenced to 25 years in prison. Since the transaction and arrest took place in Croatia, everyone agreed it best he be imprisoned there."

I took a swallow of brandy, set my glass on the table, and pulled a luscious burgundy throw from the back of the sofa. All this talk of chemical weapons intended to wipe out the United States had me feeling cold and extremely uncomfortable. Wrapping the blanket around me, I asked, "So he stayed there, locked up in a foreign country, for 25 years? Good god... What happened to the Russians?"

"They never even try to bail him out. Because they were still mixed up in the Cold War, they weren't anxious to provoke an incident, so Raines was left to rot. Basically, they disavowed him."

"Wow," I said. This was the most serious information I had ever been privy to, and I almost didn't know what to do with it all. "So... 25 years would have left him there until...what? 2010?"

"2014, actually," said Michael, his expression grim. "It wasn't long enough, in my opinion. As soon as he got out, he came back to the U.S.; he set up shop about an hour away from here and stayed low—really, really low. It wasn't until 2019 that things got messy."

"Wait—how do you know this guy? Was there a Law & Order episode or some Lifetime made-for-TV movie about him I've never seen? I don't get how you know so much about a man I've never heard of? You make it sound like you were right there, every step of the way."

Michael leaned forward, elbows on his knees, and rested his head in his hands. I reached out and placed a hand on his shoulder. He took a deep breath and mumbled, "He found out about me."

I blinked and pulled back. "Found out about you? As in—your nighttime activities?"

He chuckled but his tone was sarcastic. "Yeah, my juggling act: normal, average antique dealer by day and vampire by night."

"So *that's* what you do!" I said brightly, trying to lighten the mood. "Antiques, huh? And with you being such a historical piece yourself, that makes perfect sense!" Like I said, serious dramatic moments were not something I was good with: never sure what to do or say, no clue how to act, etc.

Michael looked up at me; his eyes were worried and strained. He was obviously haunted. "It's so bloody stupid. *I* was stupid." He sat upright and leaned back. "You don't— I was being so careful, Celie. All these years, no one ever found out about me—no one I didn't *want* to know. The only people that did—that knew the *real me*—were people

51

I revealed myself to. After nearly three centuries, I could count all of them on one hand."

"Then how did Raines find out about you? Did someone rat you out?"

"No. No, like I said, I was stupid. I was trying to help someone, just doing what was right, and...and... God, I can't BELIEVE how quickly things change..." He halted briefly, gathering himself with a swig of his brandy. "A couple of years ago, I visited the Ren Faire out in Westwood. I went every year, for nostalgic purposes. On the way to my car that night, I saw a woman getting attacked in the parking lot. It was dark out and some assholes grabbed her as she was fishing for her keys in her purse. I tried to help her, dragging the guys off her to give her a chance to get away. She kept screaming but was lucid enough to get in her car and drive off.

"Then one of the guys pulled out a gun and shot me." I gasped. "Point blank, right here," he said and pointed to the center of his abdomen. "I think the hole was probably big enough to toss a football through. Anyway, I went down, and they took off."

"Oh my god!" I exclaimed. "What did you do? Did you call the police?"

"No, that's not something you want to do when you're like me. You see, because I had fed before heading out that day, my healing abilities were perfect. About five minutes after they had disappeared, I was up and on my way to my own car to drive home—the only thing I was out of was a great shirt."

"Welp, I guess blood does the body good," I quipped, shrugging. Michael smirked at me. "Sorry, keep going," I said sheepishly.

"That's where I fucked up. Raines was there, in that parking lot. He never helped the girl, just hung around to watch with psychopathic interest—and he saw the gunshot. He saw *me*. I got up and walked away, and he returned to his little hole in the ground. He started planning that night: I was his new obsession."

"Because you survived."

"Yes. He wanted to survive gunshots, to walk away from mortal wounds. However, the main problem, Celie, was that he had dreams of making the Russians pay. They had left him with nothing but a five-by-seven-foot cell for nearly three decades. Do you know what that does to a person? Plus, he still wants to see our government suffer for the mistakes he thinks it's made. By finding out what I was, and by making himself like me, he believed he could finally see his plans through. To him, I was his golden ticket."

"Did he come after you?"

"About a month after he saw me heal, he came to my business in Bantum. I wasn't there, but my secretary, Ginny, was. Celie, I've known her for 60 years, and she knows who—and what—I am. She— She refused to tell him where I was, and there was nothing personal about me at the shop. In his anger, he took her back to his place." Michael's voice grew low and deep—seething with a hatred reserved only for Raines. "He held onto Ginny for hours, committed horrible things to her. She—she doesn't go out in public anymore."

"Oh, Michael... Oh, I'm so sorry..."

I saw his fist clench so tightly, his knuckles turn so white, I thought his hand would break purely from the force. "I take care of her, pay all her bills, bring her things when she needs them..." His voice trailed off with memories. He closed his eyes, regaining his composure by taking a deep breath.

After a minute, he continued. "I looked for him afterwards, of course, tracked him down to his hideout, but he wasn't there. He had hired six men, all ex-military like Blackwater, to guard his things. They weren't good enough, though: I moved right through them. In my rage, I took out every single one of them and burned everything down to the ground within minutes. Afterwards, I continued to feel hollow. In that moment, I knew nothing could take back that day for Ginny—or for me. For a couple of years, I researched anything and everything I could about Devlin Raines. I dug into EvRads records. I consulted with a few agents within the CIA. I even made trips to Croatia and the Russian interior to talk with his former 'associates.'"

"I'm sure you got them talking quickly, too. But how did he get into the cult business? I'm missing something there..."

"That's simple: he's a smart man. He was smart enough to understand the power of religious belief. Realizing he would need help to make his plans a reality, and being such a twisted genius, he knew he an army could be built on the backs of religious zealots. That realization led to the start of his claims that he located the new Messiah."

"That's just ridiculous," I blurted out. "People say shit like that every day and don't get cult leadership status."

"Raines is different."

"But...but tons of nuts are running around out there claiming Jesus talks to them! Dozens of ministries and preachers spend the bulk of their time telling us we're all going to hell unless we donate our life savings and follow the word of the Lord—as *they* interpret it. And they all come up with a different translation. It's just mindless nonsense."

Michael smirked. "You're right—to an extent. There are a lot of people who use religion as a tool to live happy, fulfilling lives—to do good for others. However, there are also people who get caught up in cults, hearing a message that speaks to them, or they're desperate to be saved from an unfulfilling, unhappy life. A large number of the people that follow cult leaders have an inability to make decisions. They struggle with their situation, feeling overwhelmed and lost. That kind of desperation can feel like a knife in their gut. Having someone to lead them, to tell them the choices to make while providing promises of salvation and paradise—it gives them hope and a kind of peace they couldn't feel on their own. Sometimes it's just easier, and frankly, some of them would be dead otherwise. Life is an endless struggle for them.

"Never mind that Raines knew the average person is uninformed, so he went around to state fairs, local shopping malls, anywhere he was given permission to preach. It took him about a year to get all of his followers together. They call themselves the Sons & Daughters of the Savior. There are about 1,700 of them nowadays."

"Holy Jesus," I muttered. "And they've all been after you these last couple of years?"

"Yes. I keep this place hidden from them. My curse gives me the ability to create a kind of 'fog' around this place, to block it out so normal people can't get to it."

Confused, I asked, "But you brought me here…?"

"I brought you here because they were starting to follow you, track your movements. Raines had surveillance on you for the past week, recording where you went and what you were doing. I think he was planning on taking you…to get to me." Michael stopped talking, his eyes examining my face.

He was waiting for my reaction, and only one thought came to me.

"Gee, I've never had two guys fighting over me before. How exciting."

I rolled my eyes and stood up. I needed to regain my personal space for a minute, feeling a bit stifled at the news that I was a walking target for the past *seven days*. I walked over to a bay window, staring out into the darkness for a minute. For good reason, Michael remained silent, but eventually that seemed just as overwhelming. I had to change the subject.

"So… How often do you bring girls back here, big guy?" I said sarcastically, despite my authentic curiosity. "Is this how you put the smooth moves on us ladies?"

From behind me, I heard Michael move on the sofa before saying, "I haven't had anyone here in over 60 years."

That got my attention. I turned quickly, startled to see that Michael was already moving across the room to a bookcase by the doorway. Reaching to the top shelf, he pulled down a photo album. He brought it over and handed it to me. I took it carefully, as if it was fragile and could fall apart at my touch. He returned to the sofa, collecting his brandy before retaking his seat. He took a sip as I opened the album. My reaction was instantaneous: I gasped in surprise at the first picture I saw.

Michael was in it.

"I thought that— Aren't you impossible to photograph?"

He glanced at me. "No, that's another myth. We can have our picture taken, but we come out...fuzzy? Blurry? It's like the camera can't focus on us."

"Oh," I said quietly.

As I began to go through his album, I was a little thrown by the imagery. These weren't just older pictures—they were *historical* ones. The album was brimming with black and white images of men in undershirts and handlebar mustaches, Native Americans on horseback, and railroad workers in front of Chinese laundries. There was one of Michael in the driver seat of a Model T, and one of him standing in front of a ranch out west, posing still and stoic during the late 1800s. He had photographs of himself with a large group of sailors in front of a schooner; yet one or two were of him in quiet reflection at a bar. Pictures upon pictures spanning over one hundred years were in this album. I could feel my heart skip a beat each time I flipped to another page and saw the history staring back at me.

I turned another page and found him in an army uniform staring back at me. There was a scribble on the back that said September 1942. He and another soldier were standing shoulder-to-shoulder, smiling at the cameraman, and I could see their tents and barbed wire in the background. He had been close with this man, and I asked him about the photograph.

Michael told me it was taken in England, just before they were shipped across the channel to their new command. It was his old friend, Andrew, and they had been through boot camp and a few small battles across Europe together. Andrew had dragged Michael out of a foxhole before gas was thrown in. And he had saved Andrew from a sniper when they were on the Amalfi Coast for a military operation.

A few years later, in 1948 and well after the war was over, Andrew went on his honeymoon with his new wife, Carolyn in Monterey, CA. They were driving south to spend a few nights in Pismo Beach and maybe take in the vineyards. On the way down, a large truck carrying lumber jackknifed on the Pacific Coast Highway. Andrew didn't see the truck until it was too late, and his car careened off the road and into the rocky cliffs below.

"Next to Ginny, Andrew was the last person I told," said Michael quietly.

I stopped feeling so selfish then. I knew how difficult everything must be for him. I also recognized he was putting all of his faith in me not to reject him, to not reject who and what he was. I walked over to him and sat down beside him on the sofa. I took hold of his left hand. He looked up at me, concern etched in his features, sorrow in his eyes, and without hesitating, I smiled for him. He let go of my hand and cautiously reached up to touch my face.

I let him.

His fingers were soft and gentle, like he wasn't sure if he should be touching my skin at all. His fingertips barely grazed my cheek, moving down my neck and tracing my collarbone. Brushing my auburn hair off my shoulder, he paused to feel a strand of it, and then carefully tucked it behind my ear. He didn't smile; he didn't frown. His gaze rose up to meet mine, and his eyes were serious—*hungry*.

I could feel my heart beating wildly in my chest. Something was going to happen; I could just *feel* it. There was something magical and wonderful happening. If it was a dream or a spell, I knew I was going out of control waiting for it to come to fruition.

As he watched me, I lost control, gave up the ghost, and threw caution to the wind. As if I was in one of those dream sequences in a movie, I leaned forward and kissed him. I saw it happening from a distance—an ultimate out-of-body experience. I did it urgently, feverishly, like I needed to kiss him to live. Feeling my lips touch his soft and surprisingly warm lips, I set out to discover what kissing a vampire—kissing *him*—was like, and boy was I not disappointed.

He was startled for a moment before he eagerly began kissing me back, and I had never kissed anyone with this kind of passion before. Kissing him was clearly the experience I had been waiting for my entire life. He kissed me like I was water, and he had been lost in the desert. I loved it. My entire body shivered, and I clutched his shoulders closer, feeling myself getting swept away with him—*by him*.

I felt his hands holding my head close, his breath filling me, tasting me as I tasted him in return. The smell of him, all earthy wood and warm spices, enveloped me. I was drowning in flames, drowning in our kiss, and I knew it was even more than *he* had expected.

Gradually, we pulled away from each other. I licked his lip before he pressed one slow, lingering kiss that left me feeling like I might faint all over again. I remained still, afraid to open my eyes. There was no way that kiss was real—*no way*. I had to have hallucinated because nothing had ever been like that for me—*ever*.

When I finally got the courage to open them, I found Michael looking back at me with those gorgeous steel-colored eyes of his and smiling the greatest smile I had ever seen. Holy crap, what a sexy beast! I started blushing, feeling the pink flush as it heated my cheeks, and he laughed.

I was doing that entirely too much around him.

"Uh," I said, clearing my throat. "What now?"

"First," he said, "we need to get you some sleep. It's almost 3:00am, which is seriously late for you. We can figure everything else out in the morning."

Michael rose up and held out his hand for me. I took it and let him lead me across the rug and out the doorway. I followed him up a large winding staircase to the second floor, older boards creaking beneath my bare feet. Heading down a long hallway, sconces were lit along the walls, and medieval weaponry decorated the corridor here and there. Shadows danced around the light as we passed.

At the third doorway, he stopped and opened the door for me, revealing a gorgeous bedroom, complete with an already lit fireplace and a garden-scene tapestry on the far wall to keep out the cold night air. The bed was canopied with a heavy plum-colored curtain, pulled open to reveal a raised platform bed with creamy vanilla sheets. A pale grey silk robe trimmed with white fox fur lay draped across the middle of the bed. I turned to Michael and gave him another eyebrow full.

"This will be your room...for now." He winked and lifted my hand to kiss it. Instead, he brought my wrist to his mouth and pressed his lips to the inside of it. It was intimate and unexpected, causing me to completely stop breathing.

As I stood there, my cheeks aflame, he backed out of the room.

"Goodnight," he whispered and gently closed the door.

I sucked in a breath through my gritted teeth. "Well, goddamn, that was intense. How am I gonna sleep now?"

Chapter Three

Pre-Season Training

The next few weeks would appear predominantly as a blank spot in any future autobiography. All I could remember was that I was constantly sore, bruised, and exhausted out of my mind. Not because of what you might be thinking, though. As much as I wanted more make-out sessions with Michael, I doubt I could've managed even one.

Every day started earlier than your average farmer's, and each one ended with me barely making it up the stairs for bed. Getting dressed hurt because every muscle moved like it was angry at me for giving it the exercise it hadn't seen in years. Now it seemed like all those years of repeating an infamous movie line—"I only run when chased"—were finally catching up with me.

Michael had been showing me a variety of skills to get me in shape and battle-ready. We started with different martial art moves, blending forms of Brazilian Jiu Jitsu and Muay Thai boxing, and mixing in a little Tai Chi for a rounded effect. Each day we ran through the maze outside, and every time I had to yell for Michael to come get me because I had lost my way again. I learned how to fire a shotgun and hit a target with a crossbow. I ate nothing but brilliantly prepared chicken, a variety of vegetables, and whole grains. There was no more whiskey for me, but hot baths with lots of bubbles had lovingly become my new best friend.

Ultimately, I was a miserable wretch, completely cranky, and desperate for a vacation.

My only bright side to this whole affair was that my teacher, chef, and bath preparer was the most alluring, charming, intelligent, and worldly man I had ever dreamed of. His knowledge of different cultures and languages astounded me. I held my breath every time he touched my arm to correct my aim. It was fascinating how his eyes brightened when he was happy and darkened when he was angry—or enticed. And how he looked at me? When he thought I wasn't paying attention, his gaze smoldered. I would catch it from the corner of my eye, and it was entirely more arousing than it should have been.

I felt desired—wanted—and, lord help me, was it ever a turn-on. With each passing day, I wondered what he would say or do that would cause me to lose my remaining shred of dignity and drag him to the bedroom. Hell, I had regular fantasies of having my way with him on the kitchen butcher block—cold, hard surface be damned.

Today I was all butterflies inside, just bursting with anticipation of it being the final day of training. I had spent the last couple of weeks just dying to be close to him again, but training had been all business. No distractions, he had said. We had to keep things 'professional' because he wanted to make sure that I was 'focused.' Never mind that I had a hard time focusing whenever he was around—period. I mean, really, who could focus when the embodiment of wanton abandon was positioning your hips on a firing range? Who? Tell me right now so I can slap them out of it.

For our last day, he had decided we would try a bit of sword play. I was incredibly anxious to watch him parry and thrust, and take down all of my defenses. However, it turned out I was actually a natural at fencing. Who knew?

"Ok, now I'm going to come at you from the left—good."

I spun around and slashed through the air, our swords clanging and screeching as metal slid against metal. No matter how good I was, though, I was no match for his strength. He held back as much as he could but still overpowered me with ease.

"Now defend... Parry, parry... Excellent," complimented Michael. He was stern but extremely pleased with how I had been coming along. "Good job, Celie. I think we're done. I wish we had more time for you to train, but I think we need to start taking some action."

I handed him my sword, and we started making our way back to the house. "Action?" I asked. "What kind of action?" Grabbing my bottle of water from the sidelines, I had to jog to catch up to him; he was so incredibly fast.

"The kind where you're actually going to take what you've learned and put it to use."

"What does that mean?"

He winked at me, but that was all he said about it. Sometimes he could be a real bastard about keeping secrets. Then again, he'd had decades of practice.

I continued to jog after him. I had seen some of his abilities the past few days and was definitely impressed. Michael couldn't fly, per se, but he could move so swiftly that he appeared to. His strength and agility were unrivaled, unless comparing him to a superhero, and it gave him the upper hand against absolutely anyone. He had extremely acute hearing, to the point where he could hear me upstairs mumbling when he was outside. He also had impeccable vision, giving him the ability to see a bird on a tree half a mile away—in the dark.

Vampires had a litany of amazing abilities detailed in literature and cinema. Literary accounts were filled with stories of bat transformation, swarms of rats, command of storms, and mesmerization. Other storytellers had concocted tales of their demise at silver, garlic, and crucifixes. The church was a strong opponent in most vampiric legends, as were dedicated hunters with stakes and silver crossbows. They slept during the day and only came out at night. They were sparkly and youthful, gothic and beautiful, or demonic and savagely ugly. No two stories were alike—and perhaps that was why they captured our imagination with such vivid persistency.

While some of this was true, much of it was created for sensationalism and bore no resemblance to the actual beings themselves. Most of the amazing qualities of his 'curse' were things that no one in history had ever recorded. For example, his ability to influence my dreams. I asked him about this, and he said it was like being able to play a movie for me while simultaneously editing as it played. In addition, he could read thoughts the way the average person reads a ticker at the bottom of a news channel. The thoughts came quickly to him, sometimes blending together, but giving him the advantage in a fight.

He could also use his abilities to display images, a bit like holograms but ones that appeared solid and could sometimes speak. Michael had tricked one of Devlin's people by mentally casting an image of himself turning down an alley in downtown like decoy. It was this ability that enabled him to work his way up behind the Son and take him down silently.

The Son ended up being found by some police officers the next morning.

Michael could also induce feelings—intense, hardcore, deeply erotic emotions—that compelled someone to do as he wished. He had to do this originally to feed, but it was only used as a means to an end, and he only used it as rarely as possible. Never fully comfortable with manipulating someone's will, he saw it as being too akin to slavery—something he had also never been comfortable with.

As he told me about this ability, he swore he never used this ability on me—*ever*—and that he never would. I knew it had to be true because. Like I said before, if he wanted to seduce me and take advantage of me, he could have done that already, and he hadn't.

Damn it.

Inside the house, I went upstairs to shower and change. Shortly after I had arrived, Michael had brought some of my clothes to the house, in addition to leaving a note behind for Kat to explain my whereabouts. (I just said I was away on 'vacation' for a bit.) While he put together a dinner for us downstairs, I took a hot shower. I was taking extra care to get 'read,' picking out the sexiest lingerie I had: a pair of black panties with a matching black bra. Unfortunately—or fortunately, depending on your view—Michael hadn't brought back any underthings with the intention of my seduction of him. I dried my hair and pulled it back into a loose French braid, accenting it with a bejeweled blue-green dragonfly pin near the top. Then I reached into the closet and pulled out the one dress he had brought back with him.

I had almost forgotten about this amazing dress. It had been in the back of my closet for over a year now, as I had been just waiting for an excuse to wear it. It was made of silk and ankle length. All one continuous piece, the bottom was a flowing skirt while the top was a scoop neck with thin straps over the shoulders. It was cerulean, glimmering with a shimmering purple overlay as I turned, and it fit me like the designer had used my own body as a model.

To this day, I still don't know what made him bring it from the apartment. Did he know how much of an excuse I wanted to wear it? Maybe...? He could read minds, after all.

I slipped on a pair of silver heels, fastening the small buckles that strapped around my ankles. Turning around in front of the bedroom mirror, I thought I looked quite dishy and enticing. All the right curves in all the right places; hopefully, Michael would think so, too. Once my small silver hoops were on, I spritzed myself lightly with a flowery-spice perfume. I headed out of the door and made my way down the corridor to the stairs.

In the hallway, I paused near the top of the stairwell: a painting had caught my attention. In it, there sat a family, all wearing colonial clothing. The mother and father each wore the white wigs of the period, pale faces with bright cheeks showing no obvious emotion. There were two boys and a little girl seated beneath them, all bearing sly smiles that gave away their true mischievous nature. A family crest bearing an ornately swirled letter "H" was hung above them all.

Something tickled my memory, my gaze moving back and forth between the family and the crest, the crest and the family. It suddenly dawned on me that I was looking at Michael's family. He was in this portrait, the older of the two boys, looking so peaceful. I spent another minute or two taking in his parents, his sister and brother, questions forming in my mind about them. Then I turned and hurried down the stairs.

I reached the dining room and saw Michael had set up two places at the north end of the table, complete with candlelight and a bottle of vintage Pinot Noir. *He probably bought it a year after it was made,* I thought, privately amused that I was seeing such an older man. Our meal was already laid out on silver platters and fine china: a crown pork roast, baby potatoes in a garlic and rosemary sauce, salad, and sugar snap peas steamed to perfection. I could smell freshly baked bread from the kitchen, and then Michael walked out with a basket of it, all neatly sliced and still steaming from the oven.

I smiled at him and walked over to sit down. He quickly put down the bread and came over to me, pulling out my chair for me. As I sat, he gently pushed in the chair and leaned down to me.

"You look lovely," he whispered in my ear, "and smell fantastic." Then he leaned down and placed a light kiss on my shoulder. Startled, I felt my breath catch, and it didn't come back until he began serving me. He only served himself after he had filled my plate. After pouring the wine, he walked over and sat down at the head of the table just to my left.

As we ate dinner, we talked about random things, like the Romans—geniuses or master thieves? Are trebuchets as much fun as they look? We also both agreed we would never want to meet an anaconda in the Amazon or a great white shark in South Africa.

However, we didn't talk about what I so badly wanted to ask him about—his family. What were they like? What happened to them? Were any of them vampires? Were any of them still around? Still alive?

My thoughts and questions must have escaped outward because Michael abruptly stopped talking mid-sentence. He looked over at me and, with a wistful smile murmured, "All you had to do was ask."

I glanced down. "I'm so sorry."

"Don't be." He reached out and gently tilted my chin up so I could see he wasn't mad. "It's natural you would be curious about them—and about me..."

"You, you haven't said much about yourself."

"Then I will remedy that, love."

In my brain, I began doing cartwheels. *He called me 'love'!*

Michael began by telling me all about his father, Jonathan. He had worked as a sort of merchant's accountant, handling the inventory and receipts for various shipping and trading companies. His mother, Cressida, also worked but more as a hobby. She had a small entrepreneurship helping design the interiors of many upper-class homes. His parents were both independent and freethinkers. They chose not to own slaves, instead choosing to pay a fair wage to anyone who worked for them. Each of them spoke freely at council meetings and expressed a true interest in furthering the endeavors of entertainers and artisans.

Michael had assisted his father, mostly running errands, but also handling the bulk of communications between his father and the merchants. His younger brother and sister—Samuel and

Lavinia—were very clever and playful, but much too young to make any contributions to the family. Michael had lived a very comfortable life, never wanting for anything. While his family wasn't part of the plentiful aristocracy, they were most definitely not poor.

"Then one day, *she* showed up," Michael ground out, unable to contain his anger.

"Who is 'she'?" I asked, knowing I would hate the answer.

His voice dripping with venom and contempt, Michael snarled, "Amelia Langston."

Yup—just the name sounded poisonous.

"Men found her beautiful, mysterious, like a trophy they would kill others to win. They were always seeking her bed and being consistently denied. All the women envied her, wanting to be as fashionable, as desirable as she was. Every woman wanted her husband to look at them the way he looked at her, but more importantly, women wanted to *be* her. She was smart, clever, and talented in everything she attempted: archery, riding, singing... There was nothing she couldn't accomplish

"On top of all of this, she was more wealthy than God and just as wrathful."

Oh yeah, I hated her.

"But she was cold, unfeeling, playing with everyone like a cat with a mouse. She manipulated and deceived anyone she wanted—lied and betrayed everyone. Blackmail was a favorite weapon of hers, and she was completely indifferent to the devastation she caused. All in all, she was the most evil, vile, and horrendously cruel woman that I have ever encountered."

I sat on the edge of my seat, hanging onto his every word. Cautiously, I asked, "Did she— Were you ever— What did she do to your family, Michael?"

"You must understand something: Amelia was cunning and an excellent strategist. She had a true head for business. That's what my father saw in her. He assisted her in ordering several shipments of spices and arranging insurance policies with various gentlemen throughout the city. Unbeknown to him, she took out abnormally high policies on the shipments, ones that far exceeded their value, by claiming there was more on board than there truly was. Then she made deals with various captains to 'alter their courses due to bad weather.'"

"'Alter their courses'? What does that mean?"

"It means she diverted cargo to high-risk areas. She hired rogue pirates to attack the ships, pillaging and burning them into the sea, and leaving her to collect on the insurance policies. She was literally profiting from profiteers and the financial ruin of others." Michael stopped talking, staring off into his memories, his eyes growing dark. "Many men lost their lives in the Atlantic and their homes in the colonies because of her plotting and scheming. She simply reaped the rewards..." he whispered.

This was something that greatly disturbed Michael. Afraid to startle him, I spoke quietly. "Did your father know?"

He blinked, as if waking from a trance. Turning to me, he apologized. "I was lost in thought."

Giving him a small smile, I replied, "You've told me so much. If you don't want to talk about this anymore, that's okay with me." His right hand lay on the table, clenched in a fist. I placed my left hand over it, covering his with my warmth. "I mean it. You won't hurt my feelings."

He took a big breath, exhaling slowly. "No. In actuality, I *need* to talk about it. I— I never did..." I felt his hand relax beneath mine. His voice tinged with sadness, he added, "I wanted to put this behind me, so I tried to forget about it. Now I'm seeing that not dealing with it doesn't make it actually go away." He looked down. "You can't grieve something that's put away in a box, hidden from sight."

Placing his other hand on top of mine, he continued his story. "I never had to tell my father what people were saying about Amelia. He was hearing the rumors firsthand. The first two times the ships were attacked, the losses appeared to be just terrible accidents. The other captains were devastated by the sinking of the Persephone and the Selene. However, my father caught on when the Pulchra Regina (Beautiful Queen), which had always stopped in Charlestown, South Carolina, never did," he said.

"What happened to it?"

"Another crew spotted it circling a Bahamian island. That was the clue: it should have gone straight past on its way back from Jamaica. The rumors had been swirling for weeks, but my father took this as gospel that something was amiss. He pulled all the logs from previous shipments and reviewed the courses the captains had plotted before. Not a single captain had so drastically diverted from their plotted route before. Plus, they were claiming storms had been the cause, but no other ships reported encountering the foul weather.

"My father took Amelia aside and told her what he was hearing. She pretended not to know but acknowledged she had heard similar 'concerning stories.' She promised to keep her eyes open for anything suspicious, and that appeared to be the end of it. However, six months later, another ship was lost, and my father confronted her again. This time, she tried to bribe him, get him to keep his mouth shut about the entire ordeal. He refused and told her he was going to see the Governor."

"And I'm guessing she didn't like that idea," I stated.

Michael grunted. "She came to our home one night—*late*—while Samuel and Lavinia were sleeping. I was upstairs, sorting through papers for my father, when she arrived. He told me to wait while he spoke with her in our study. I heard them arguing, voices raised, and I remember being worried they would wake up my brother and sister." Michael let out a single, soft laugh. "When I think of that, knowing what I know now, its such a trivial thing." Angrier, he whispered, "I should have woken them, taken them away, and left our home far, far behind."

"You didn't know, Michael. You have to stop punishing yourself. Seriously, you don't have to tell me anymore. This is upsetting you, and I—"

He ignored me.

"All of a sudden, I realized I heard nothing at all. Despite my father's instruction, I came down the stairs to see what was happening."

I could see that Michael was lost in time. His words were giving his memories new life, and he was sinking deeper into them, reliving them as he sat with me. I wanted to comfort him, but I wasn't sure how. This was well and above any experience I could ever expect to have, so I chose to sit and listen, to be there for him when he resurfaced from his past.

"I walked into the study, and that's how I found the demon bent over my father, drinking from him. His eyes turned to glass in front of me. My mother was on the settee already dead: she was drained, and her neck was broken.

"Before I could move, Amelia was upstairs and had killed my siblings. She was older than I am now, and time had left her jaded, detached. Murdering children was the least of her sins. All I can hope for is that they were both asleep when she did it, that they felt nothing in those final moments."

I was completely without words. This was worse than anything I had imagined happening to his family. I had no idea what I would have done in that kind of situation. Without knowing what to say, I began caressing the back of his hand, rubbing slowly back and forth with my thumb in an attempt to be reassuring. Michael kept going.

"She came back downstairs, blood smeared all over her face and clothing, and she just—she smiled at me. I saw her teeth, her pale skin, her glowing green eyes: I nearly went insane. I knew what it all meant—what she truly was. I had heard rumors from immigrants that had come over from the old world. Aware of her true nature, I was both petrified and doubly ashamed that I to be.

"But I didn't have time to be afraid. She used her mental abilities to seduce me, to coerce me into saying I wanted to be like her. She took me right in front of my dead mother and father. As they lay in their still warm blood, she killed me and gave me this curse—and the whole time I hated her. I hated her for everything she had done, everything she had taken from me—from my *family*... Weeks later, I escaped her abuse and torture.

"After several months had passed, winter had arrived, and she found me in an alleyway." He scoffed. "She tried to convince me that she had wanted me all along and that my parents were just business. She tried to get me to come back with her—to be in her *bed*. We fought, and I ended up killing her."

Michael sighed. "I know she's dead, you know. I know she's not coming back. But not a single speck of my hate for her has diminished. I hate her now just as much as I did that same night." Michael looked over at me, his brow knit in confusion. "Do you think that will ever go away?"

I gave myself a moment, wanting to get my words just right. "Maybe," I replied softly. "Anger like that—anger that I can't even begin to imagine—I think it takes a lot of effort to move past it. For some people, it fades with time. It's like there's a loss of connection to that moment. I know you won't ever forgive her, and you won't forget what happened; however, one day you might wake up, and it won't hurt as much as the day before."

"I hope so," he murmured. He bent down, resting his forehead on our overlapping hands. I heard him sigh again, and with one hand still free, I reached over and began stroking his hair. I tried to pour all of my caring and feeling for him into each pass, and I waited patiently for him to let the anger go, giving him as much time as he needed to gather himself.

Eventually, we finished dinner and bid each other good evening. It didn't feel right to pursue anything after such an intense reveal. I went to my room, changed into a white t-shirt, and climbed into bed. Lying there in the dark, I thought about how much I still didn't know, how much danger he had been in, and the sheer level of insanity Michael had been through. Would I go through those things? Would I ever learn all there is to know about Michael? I could tell I was falling in love with him, and I was scared to death about everything that meant.

'*There's so much I don't know....*'

I fell into a restless sleep that night.

Imagine my surprise when, late the next morning, I jerked awake from a wonderfully peaceful dream to someone knocking on the front door of the house. I groaned and put my pillow over my head. *Let Michael get it*, I thought. *I'm going back to sleep.*

Then I sat up quickly.

"No one should be able to do that," I whispered out loud to myself. I flung my legs out of bed and reached for some nearby black sweatpants. The knocking continued downstairs. I ran out of the room, pulling my messy hair back into a top knot as I rushed down the stairs.

I glanced around the front hall and into the sitting room. There was no sign of Michael. Cautiously, with all of my instincts telling me something was really wrong, I moved to the other side of the door and tried to peek outside from behind a curtain.

Two people stood on the porch, a man and a woman, both dressed in starchy white button-down shirts and black dress pants with patent leather black shoes. I let out a sigh of exasperation, amazed that even the Jehovah's Witness crowd could find this house and come calling. The man was very short, with dark brown hair, his face fresh and clean shaven. He was very boyish looking, and he may have actually been a boy; however, he seemed cold and lacking any emotion—something that comes from a hard life filled with rotten experiences. His eyes were incredibly dark and empty, like shark eyes. On closer inspection, I could see that despite his boyish looks, he was older than he appeared.

The woman was another story. Well over six feet tall, she had light, almost white-blonde hair pulled back in a severe frizz-free bun. Not a single strand was out of place. Her pointed nose and sunken cheeks gave her an altogether skeletal look, her dark eyes like small voids leading into her brain. Her clothes hung off her frame, and they were much more wrinkled and dingy than I realized at first glance.

Both were extremely pale, and neither wore any facial expression, remaining stoic. Neither of them carried any brochures or books, either. I also couldn't see any evidence of crosses or crucifixes with them, which was puzzling for door-to-door religion peddlers.

In short, both gave me the creeps.

Yet, despite my extensive training with Michael to fight the bad people coming for us, and despite their bizarre appearance—on what was supposed to be a *hidden* property's doorstep—I was a complete moron and opened the door.

"Hi! Are you guys here to offer religious assistance?" They just stared blankly, and it reminded me of Stepford wives. "Well listen, I hate to waste your time, but the devil is already in this house. We're chock full of everything we need for our next sacrifice, but thanks for stopping by!"

I tried to close the door, but Blondie stretched out her hand and stopped it, her palm flat against the door. Slowly, her eyes moved from staring straight ahead to looking right at me, borderline *through me*, and a fake smile crept across her face. It didn't reach her eyes, which were somehow darker than before. Her teeth were extremely white and gleaming in the daylight, reminding me of false teeth.

"Miss Moore, I presume?" Her voice was flat, with a steady, monotone inflection.

Caught off guard, I mumbled, "No, you've got the wrong house." She had to be one of the cult members. I tried to shut the door again, fear kicking me in the gut like a stallion. It didn't budge—and that made my anxiety even worse.

Blondie arched an eyebrow at my response. "Actually, I believe we have the correct house."

"No, totally wrong. This is the Hill house. I'm actually just babysitting for them. In fact, they'll be back this afternoon if you want to just stop by later." I casually leaned into the door, trying to close it again, but it still wouldn't move.

Was her arm made of steel?

Billy Boy leaned over and whispered something into her ear. Blondie turned and sternly told him 'no.' He began to pout, evidently disappointed by her answer. She turned her attention back to me.

"Miss Moore, we are here to collect you. If you don't want to come quietly, that is not a problem for us. However, you may be less likely to enjoy the trip."

"I'm telling you," I replied hoarsely, "I'm not this Moore chick you keep asking for."

Blondie took a step forward, and I retreated to match, each of us keeping a hand on the door. She smirked. "If you aren't her, then why are you afraid? Hmm?" She scoffed. "You reek of fear."

"You—you better leave. Now," I said with a shaky voice, trying to put up a false bravado. Who was I kidding? A few weeks of training and my dumb ass thought I was ready? Ha! If all these Sons and Daughters were like Blondie here, I didn't have a chance in hell.

"Foolish girl—very foolish. Didn't he tell you about us?"

"What?!" I said as a mixture of confusion welled up within my fear. Now I was feeling extra panicky. Where the hell was Michael?

"He's gone, you know. He has left you here—all alone," said Blondie, and I flinched. Had she read my thoughts? "Yes, Miss Moore. You heard me correctly."

Now I was terrified. She took another step forward and pushed the door open wider. Then her smile disappeared, and her voice became low and very, very menacing. "You should be afraid. We've come here to take you with us. Now let's go."

I couldn't believe what this skinny Amazonian bitch was telling me. Michael, the man/vampire I was falling in love with, was gone. He left me here—*alone*. What a cosmically sized asshole! Now two of those radical, insane people working for that Devlin guy were here to kidnap me. Great—just fucking peachy.

I did the only thing that I could think of under the circumstances: clenching my fists in anger, I told Billy Boy and Blondie to fuck off and ran into the house. I charged up the stairs, grabbing a beautifully sharp scimitar off the wall as I reached the second-floor hallway. Then I scurried into my room and bolted the door shut. The trunk at the foot of the bed was heavy, so I dragged it toward the doorway. It howled and screeched as it drove sharp lines into the wood floors, but I didn't care. I shoved it against the door as close and tight as I could, hoping it would be a good barrier.

Starting to back up a few feet, I paused. Not a single sound came from outside my room. However, all of my years of movie experience told me that didn't mean crap, and I started moving again, silently backing all the way into the dark belly of my closet. Continuing to feel exposed, I turned around and carefully climbed up the built-in shelving until I was at the very top. Fortunately, they were solid wood and deep, receding a couple of feet into the wall. Tucking myself in, I remembered the double doors and reached out, pulling them closed. From there, I waited.

A few moments passed before I heard them, their heavy steps just outside the door. They were in the hallway, checking the rooms one by one. I could feel the doors being slammed shut, the impact coming through the wall at my back.

In my hiding place, I was trying not to go into full-fledged shock. I was still reeling from the fact that they even found the damned house. Now my panic mode was at Def-Con 12 that they could *enter* it. How did they find it? Why were they able to get through his fog? Were there more of them outside? Didn't Michael have more defenses set up?

And most importantly, *where the fuck was he?*

As if I had mentally screamed his name, I blinked and Michael was in the closet, appearing right in front of me, standing just inside the double doors. He looked like he had been inside with me the whole time. I shrieked, jerked backwards, and bumped my head on the ceiling of the closet. He held up a hand and put a finger to his lips, telling me to be quiet.

I gave him a different finger.

How dare he show up now and try to tell me what to do! I wanted to produce my sword and spear him to the closet door. However, I didn't think I could wrench my fingers away from the hilt: I was gripping it like a bull rider holding onto the bull rope.

You have some goddamn nerve showing up in my closet, you jerk! I poured all my anger, fear, and frustration into my thought, emphasizing the 'jerk' part. I was still panicked but now more furious at him than anything else.

He had the audacity to roll his eyes. *Look, I'll explain it all later. Stop being a hardass and get down off that shelf.*

No. You left me, I ground out mentally. *And I'm not going anywhere near Blondie. That bitch is freaky.*

You have to come down here and fight. Hiding won't stop them. You need to face your fears.

I clenched my jaw and stayed put. I may be a hardass, but I was still pissed off at him for abandoning me.

Damn it, Celie. I'm sorry. I had to take care of Ginny. I hadn't visited her in almost two weeks, and I needed to make sure she was alright.

Uh-oh. Pack my bags; I was going on a guilt trip. My body instantly relaxed as my shame overtook my anger.

Michael's tone was serious. *They won't ever stop looking for you, so get your ass down here. You can't hide in my closet for the rest of your life.* He gently pushed the door open, then turned around to wait for me.

I wanted to be stubborn. I wanted to stay up there just out of spite, but of course I knew he was right. I couldn't keep hiding in the closet for the rest of my life. Without saying anything—mostly because my pride wouldn't let me—I climbed down until I was standing in front of him. He eyed my sword and nodded before stepping forward. He wrapped an arm around me—

Suddenly, we were downstairs in the front hall. I pushed him back and held him at arm's length, gawking at him in amazement. *What the hell? Since when could you do* that?

Michael looked down at me and smiled. *I can't tell you all of my secrets. How else could I still surprise you from time to time?*

I socked him in the arm, and he feigned like I hurt him, giving me a small pout. I stuck my tongue out at him before we both turned towards the staircase.

Devlin's two visitors were halfway down the stairs, but things had changed. Blondie had on that same fake, twisted smile from the doorway, but her teeth weren't as white as I first thought. Actually, they were stained, and very crooked, and some of them were a bit pointed—as if they had been sharpened. Her eyes were different, too: darker, blacker, the whites all but disappeared.

And Billy Boy? That creepy kid had appeared to have gotten shorter, stockier, and—wow—kind of hunched over? He had looked somewhat like a typical sitcom kid before, but now... He looked like the lovechild of those kids with Igor. He still had the creepy eyes trained on me, but they were bigger and rounder—and all black like Blondie's.

I never mentioned how eyes like that scared me. I had a constant fear of sharks my whole life, mostly because of their teeth—and their ability to shred a hunk of meat like it was paper. But shark eyes were probably the creepiest eyes on earth: cold, dead, lifeless. They bore no mercy, showed no compassion, and they were the last thing you saw before you were eaten alive.

There was no love lost between me and sharks.

Seeing them both with those black, soulless eyes, I was scared to death. Didn't heroes always say to "hold your fire until you see the whites of their eyes?" Well, what if the bad guys didn't *have* 'whites' anymore? I was floundering in fear, absolutely gripped by it, and I just needed someone to tell me to stand fast—to have courage.

Michael nudged me. "Courage, Celie..."

I smirked at him.

Blondie and Billy Boy reached the bottom of the stairs—and promptly disappeared.

"I was afraid they would do that," said Michael, and he yanked me forward, dragging me across the hall. I glanced over my shoulder and saw Billy Boy and Blondie reappear where we had just been standing.

"Oh crap..." I muttered. I stopped letting him drag me and ran past him into the study.

Chapter Four

As Powerful as My Own

Just like I figured, Billy Boy was desperate to pummel me, and he came loping fast on my heels. I spun around and gave him a roundhouse into his gut, causing him to double over. But like any uniquely powered villain, his head whipped up, and he grinned like the fun was really about to begin. He swung out and nailed me on my jaw. I heard the crack, and my vision flickered. I fell backward, my only weapon flying out of my hand and across the floor as my body landed on the hard wood with a thunk.

He walked over and grabbed my right leg, proceeding to drag me back out to the hallway. I reached out, desperately seeking anything to hold onto, fingers clawing and arms flailing. The door frame came into view, and I stretched my left arm out. Grabbing it firmly, I rolled onto my side and quickly found purchase with my other hand. Realizing I was snagged on something, Billy Boy yanked, and I couldn't help but shout in pain as they were wrenched. The last thing I wanted was for them to come out of their sockets; yet I managed to hold on for dear life. He dropped me and started coming around. I think he expected to just pull the door frame off the wall—with me still attached.

I used that instant to roll to my stomach and push up, scrambling to my feet. I didn't hesitate, dashing away from him and heading right for my sword across the room. I snatched it up from the floor and swung around to brace myself for his attack.

It never came: Billy Boy was gone.

"Damn it, not again," I muttered, turning this way and that. "I don't need this crap; like, I *really* don't." I spun in circles looking for him. "Using magic is just supremely—"

I was about to say 'unfair' when he showed up just to the side of me. Of course, I had been turning in the opposite direction, so I didn't catch him in time. His arms wrapped around me—not just once but twice—lifting me off the ground and squeezing like a python. I instantly freaked out. *How the hell does this guy have arms that long?* No way was I dying because of this crazy, contortionist hunchback!

I struggled against him, but it had little effect. Every time I took a breath, his hold grew tighter and tighter. I felt his hot breath on the back of my neck, and I gagged at the intimacy of it. Using my head—because it was the only weapon I had available—I slammed back into his nose.

Apparently, Billy Boy had a fragile face. His nose wasn't as flexible as the rest of him, crunching violently on impact. In an instant, he released me, his arms unwinding from around my torso and writhing in the air. I dropped back down to the floor on one knee and spun to my left. Hands firmly on the hilt of my sword, I brought it up and sliced down in an arc, cutting open his belly.

He screamed, and it was the most horrifying sound I had ever heard: wailing, layered, *inhuman.* Bursting into bright green flames, his entire body was swallowed whole by it: I had never seen anything like it before. His corpse stumbled around the room like a marionette, mouth hanging open as his scream continued to pour out of it. I scrambled away from him, terrified of what was happening. All of a sudden, Billy Boy's jerky dance ceased, his screaming stopped, and his body collapsed. No longer lit by flame, it burst into ashes as it came in contact with the floor. In seconds, a charred stain was all that remained on the hard wood.

I was out of breath from the effort. My body was running purely on adrenaline. I quickly looked around for Michael, frantic to find him, and a fierce shriek caught my attention. Rushing to the doorframe that had saved my life mere moments earlier, I stumbled to a jagged halt.

In the hall, at the bottom of the staircase, Michael and Blondie were in a fist fight for the ages. Hair, flesh, and blood were spraying everywhere. I had only seen Michael heal from cuts from my sword, but now I was witnessing him as he fended off claws and teeth. Every tear of his skin, every break of a bone, he merely grunted and continued to fight like a valiant—and deadly—knight.

I rushed toward them, fully prepared to help kick her ass, but before I could reach them, my legs were knocked out from underneath me. I landed on my right hip, throbbing pain radiating through my pelvis, and glanced at my legs to see what happened. Around the back of my ankles and calves were wounds like barbed wire would make. With blood leaking down my heels, I looked around in confusion. When did Michael put booby traps in here?

That's when I saw what I had missed. Mixed in among their shuffling feet was a sickly orange tail, studded with triangular barbs, swishing across the floor. I followed along the length of it with my eyes and saw it was attached to Blondie—and that wasn't the only change to her ensemble. As I watched, her jaw grew, bones cracking as it extended and its gape ever widening. In seconds, it was open larger than Michael's entire head, with row after row of roughly angled, sharply pointed teeth: I flinched as I saw them graze his skin. She didn't pause for an instant either, striking at him with her tail, trying to bite him when he was distracted by its biting sting. To make things creepier and far more horrific, she was hissing, and it was more like a cockroach than a snake.

Blondie was a freak-show attraction to the Nth degree.

Casting her lifeless eyes in my direction, she tried to stab at me again with her tail, the very tip speared like an indigo dagger. As her new appendage struck at me again, I flung myself out of the way. It slammed into the staircase and ripped through the steps. Sword still in hand, I swung and sliced the very tip off of it. She screeched, backing away from Michael and hurriedly pulling her tail in close. Hissing, she twitched her stump of a tail and gnashed her teeth. She was something from a nightmare—a Clive Barker creation—and I was all too eager to wake up.

Michael reached into the waistband of his pants and pulled out a silver dagger I hadn't seen before. Celtic and Nordic markings adorned the blade, with simple leather wrapped around the hilt for a firm, solid grip. It was simple and basic but intense and deadly, too. Wielding it like it was an extension of his arm, he slashed diagonally downward through her defenses, cutting her open like she was made of paper. Before I knew what he was planning, he twisted his hand, and plunged it upward into her chest, piercing her organs—her black heart—and striking her deep.

Echoing a cry like that of Billy Boy's, her scream carried through the house, ringing in my ears and clawing behind my eyes. Michael took advantage of Blondie's vulnerability and slashed across her throat, causing her agonizing melody to be abruptly silenced. Also, like Billy Boy, she burst into a blaze of green, her body consumed by it as it fed on her fleas. I shielded my eyes from it, climbing higher on the staircase to escape her. She swirled and slid across the floor of the hall in a twisted, macabre ballet, and I couldn't help but wonder if she used to be a dancer. Just as my own enemy had done, she soon became a pile of black ash.

I plunked down on the bottom step. Dazed, I wasn't even aware that I bent my legs and brought my knees up to my chin. Wrapping my arms around them to hold them close, I glanced at Michael. He was standing still, breathing heavily and staring at the spot where Blondie had—died? Disintegrated? He looked up at me and nodded his head, as if acknowledging my help and my efforts.

My brain went into analytical mode, trying to process what had just happened; it was the only way I could deal with it. I had to have answers, an explanation, and my instincts told me Michael wouldn't give it to me. I threw myself as far out of the situation as possible, removing my feelings from it, and focusing on the facts. If the cast of a forensic television show had been available, I would've used them to go from top to bottom with DNA sampling and spectral analyzing. I would've had an unsub profile in minutes. What were those things? Were they really sent by Devlin? What if I hadn't been trained? Is this really what I was up against? I was certain Michael knew more about them, but I wanted to be assertive and investigate for myself. Maybe I could find something about them outside...

In a millisecond, I was up and striding across the hall.

"Clean it up, would you?" I told Michael as I passed him, pointing to the pile on the floor. From the corner of my eye, I saw his jaw drop. Reaching the front door, I grabbed the doorknob and threw it wide open. I stepped out into the sunlight and onto the front steps.

Scanning the circular driveway for evidence of how they got here, I immediately saw what *wasn't* there: no car, no motorcycles—not even a damned bicycle. These were definitely *not* Jehovah's Witnesses. I felt so stupid, so dumb: I never should have opened that damn door.

I walked down the steps and out across the gravel. Passing the fountain, I made my way to the gate, thinking there might be clues there, expecting to find something that might clue me in on everything. Nothing was there: no footprints, no tire tracks, and not a single sign of forced entry.

Did they hack his security system? No, *that* was impossible. He was using vampire abilities. There was no 'system'—only magic.

I turned around and saw Michael standing by the front door, watching me. I walked back over to him, looking around the property as I went. Snippets of details were falling into place with every step I took, until the whole picture was clear in my mind. Heading back up the steps, I stopped directly in front of him and unleashed my venom.

"This was you, wasn't it? You did this! You brought them here as some kind of...of a.what? A test? You were testing me?"

Michael stayed silent, and I took that as my answer. I shoved him as hard as I could—which only moved him about an inch. I might as well have been trying to move a mountain. "You superior asshole! I could've been killed! You thought what—'Oh, this'll be fun!'—right? 'She'll be fine, and if she dies, oh well.' You *colossal* jerk!" I shouted and stomped into the house.

"Celie!" he called out after me. I could hear his steps as he followed me inside. "You needed this!"

I spun around, incredulous at hearing the words coming from his gorgeous mouth. "I *needed* this? Are you insane? Why in my right fucking mind would I need some terrifying attack like *this*?"

"You did," he insisted. "I had to find out if you were ready. You did great, by the way. I promise you there was no danger. None whatsoever." When I continued to gape at him, he added, "I swear you would never have been hurt. Never."

My fury didn't accept his rationale. Straightening my spine, I turned back around and ran up the stairs to my room, slamming the door shut. I flopped onto my bed, lying on my belly. I was completely exhausted, confused, and very, very frustrated. On the other side of the door, he was calling to me, asking me to listen to him, and telling me it was done with the best of intentions. All I wanted to do was open the door back up and slam it closed on his head. At least he was respecting my privacy and not porting into the room to talk it out. I kept still, focusing on my breathing as I waited for him to leave me alone. I needed time to process this, to release my anger, and to just breathe. I couldn't do it right now, and I definitely couldn't do it with him in the vicinity.

A few hours later, I was calm, collected, and not quite as eager to punch a hole through something. I had changed into a pair of dark bootcut jeans with a white t-shirt and black leather ankle boots. The only jewelry I wore was a simple silver necklace with a Celtic cross pendant. I was comfortable, and that was all that mattered at the moment. My hair was pulled back into a simple ponytail, and I felt it swing from side to side as I walked out of my room and down the hallway.

At the top of the stairs, I paused to see if Michael was in the hallway. I didn't see him or any piles of ashes. I leaned over the railing and looked into the study—nothing there either. *Good*, I thought, *because I don't want to have to walk past any of that.* I went down to the first floor and walked around back towards the kitchen. I was starving and ready to eat twelve footlong club sandwiches if they were available.

When I reached the kitchen, it was also empty. I opened the fridge and rummaged through to find some leftover roast chicken. I took it out, cut off some slices, then concocted a brilliantly simple—yet satisfying— sandwich complete with lettuce, tomato and mayo on sourdough. I sat down at the table with my plate, and as I started to eat my sandwich, I noticed a note propped up against the vase of flowers standing in the middle of the table.

First, I should point out that we didn't have a vase of flowers the day before. Second, the flowers were my favorite: peonies. I leaned over them to inhale the wonderful smell, casually touching the ruffled, velvet petals. I admired them for a moment before snatching up the note and reading it quickly.

Cecelia, I am sorry.

Despite what you may think, I never intended to hurt you, or for you to get hurt. I had to be sure that you were ready before we went after Devlin. The last thing I wanted was for you to find out you needed more time in the middle of an actual confrontation.

The two creatures we fought were actually lower-level demons I summoned, and they were much stronger than anything you would face in Devlin's ranks. They were fully controlled by me. While they did cause you some pain, they wouldn't have been able to do anything worse. I simply wanted to make sure that what was in front of you would appear real and threatening. Anything less and neither of us would know if you could handle yourself.

Again, please don't hate me. I couldn't bear it. I only wanted to make sure that you were ready and capable.

If I lost you to Devlin, I don't know what I would do...

~Michael~

Hmm, I thought. *That's not a bad apology.*

But I could do better, I suppose?

I spun around and Michael was sitting on the kitchen counter, watching me. He was leaning forward, his hands on the edge of the countertop, braced upright by his bare arms. Barefoot, he wore jeans and a buttery soft, denim blue t-shirt. He had an unfair advantage over me: the short sleeves only served to accentuate his arm muscles and make his steel eyes more blue than normal. I felt my knees go weak—even sitting down.

"You know you could've just told me you were sorry instead of writing this note. Not that I hate the note—it's a great touch."

He smirked. "You weren't exactly listening to me at the time."

"Fine—that's fair." I sighed before crossing my arms over my chest. I gave him that stance that every woman knows, the one that demanded—no, *commanded*—an apology. "Well, I'm listening now. This is as good a time as any. Fire away."

He hopped down and stepped forward. He placed a hand on each of my upper arms. Looking me right in the eyes, he simply said, "I'm sorry, Celie."

I pursed my lips at him, like I was trying to decide if I would accept his apology. But before I realized what was going to happen, he finalized his apology by leaning down and kissing me.

I froze, shocked that he was finally kissing me after all this time. It felt like forever since that night in his study, and he had both hands on either side of my face, his lips soft and warm and achingly sweet. After a moment, my shock wore off, and I began to kiss him back. I felt myself sigh, overcome and weak, that I could finally touch him—and be touched *by* him. I trembled from the sheer pleasure of it, slanting my head slightly so he could deepen our kiss. He did so *eagerly*, and I was in heaven. Using the tip of my tongue, I traced it across his upper lip. He groaned and kissed me again, his hands sliding down my arms, his thumbs caressing my skin. The whole while, he tortured me with his tongue, teasing me with hints of what else he might use it for.

Then I made a mistake, just a teeny, tiny one.

In my hunger for him, I nicked myself on one of his teeth. Instantly, I pulled away, and Michael froze, quiet and unmoving. I stared at him and saw something begin to glow in his eyes. Iridescent, it started soft and low, getting brighter with every passing second. I watched him swallow, and my heart began to pound. I didn't know what my blood would do to him. Would he attack me? Would he mesmerize me and drain me? What had I done?

Suddenly, I felt tremendous heat—searing, scorching heat—like I was thrust into a furnace. I began to ache between my thighs, tingling and feeling more aroused than I had ever been in my life—or any previous one. Carnal, wanton thoughts swept through my brain, images of us in all the ways I had never known, his fingers on my skin, his tongue licking my—

I knew I couldn't stop what was going to happen...

...and I didn't want to.

With Michael's desire rushing over me, I was instantly desperate to have him. I rose quickly out of my chair, and we rushed at each other in a desperate need for contact. I practically climbed onto him, pulling him toward me, and throwing a leg around him. I kissed him like he was air that I needed to breathe. His arms came around me, embracing me in a way that I was fully encircled in his arms. A growl came from him, low and deep within his throat—like the way an animal would with its mate.

Nothing could have turned me on more.

I could feel my pulse, hear it in my ears, and sense the blood rushing in my veins; I knew he did, too. His arms released me, and I felt him slide his hands down my back, then further still until he had my ass cheeks in his hands. He pulled me closer, and I rubbed up against him.

"Oh god, I want this," I whispered in his ear right before I took his earlobe into my mouth. That completely pushed him over the edge. The next thing I knew, he had backed us up against the table. He reached behind me and swept everything off it, then he laid me on top of it, his mouth on mine, practically devouring me.

Our bodies were melding together, and I lost any restraint I had left. Sensing his own control only seconds away from breaking, I didn't waste a moment. I took hold of his shirt and began dragging it up and over his head; he was only too eager to let me. I tossed it to the floor and held him back for a minute. I just wanted to look at him, to take him in with my eyes. Good lord, this man was unbelievably sexy. His broad shoulders, his muscular chest, his tight stomach that tapered down into that gorgeous V... I sighed, letting my hands slide down his arms, feeling every muscle tighten with unreleased sexual tension.

With a sinful smile full of promises I knew he would keep, he stood up and reached for my jeans. As he unbuttoned them, I began anxiously taking my shirt off. As soon as I could, I let them fall away, and I watched him as he began pulling my jeans off my legs, one by one. He didn't rush back to me, though; instead, Michael moved up my body slowly, pressing tender kisses to my calves, my thighs, and my navel as he went. Each one was intense and intimate, as if he was worshipping my body, and every touch of his lips seemed to brand me as his. He kissed the tops of my breasts and along my collarbone, his large hands holding me at my waist. Very quickly, my bra disappeared.

Michael never stopped touching me—he just changed direction. He teased my breasts with his tongue. I couldn't stop sliding my hands over his back, his shoulders, all muscled and smooth. On a whim, I scratched my nails down his back, and I felt him smile against me. He began to drag his tongue down my stomach, swirling my navel and nipping at my skin. I braced myself as he grabbed my hips and held me still.

Then my sexy, ungodly vampire started dragging my panties off with his teeth. Soon they were also at his feet, and before I could do anything, he had his head between my thighs: parting, tasting, licking. He flattened his tongue against my cunt, slowly dragging it up and then flicking it over my clit. His hands held me still, until he brought one down and placed his palm against the inside of my thigh. Gently, intentionally, he pushed my leg out and up, then he came closer, draping my leg over his shoulder. Seconds later, my other leg was over his other shoulder, and he was drowning me in sensations: mine and his. The things this man could do with his tongue had clearly been taught to him by the devil. There was no way to even begin to describe them. His tongue tasted me, his fingers caressed me and dove into me, and I knew I was losing myself in his arms.

I felt myself beginning to ascend, climbing higher and higher, not wanting it to stop, hoping he would *never stop*... Then I burst, erupting into a thousand tiny fragments of myself, shouting his name and thinking I might never be put back together. I felt myself falling from the heavens, and he was the one who caught me. I may have been shattered, but I wasn't broken—not by a long shot. I reached forward, grabbing the waist band of Michael's jeans and pulled myself up. Seizing his belt, I started unfastening it as he took my right breast into his mouth. I undid his pants and shoved them down off his hips—and I was not met with disappointment. I pulled down on his boxers and captured the hard, rigid length of him in my hand. Beginning to stroke him, I loved how his teeth grazed my nipples as I did.

We toyed with each other—squeezing, stroking, savoring—until neither of us could take another minute of separation. Standing between my legs, he grabbed both sides of my hips as I clutched the table edge. Slowly, torturously, he pushed his cock inside of me. He fit me perfectly, like the gods designed us that way. I could feel him all over me, inside of me, surrounding me with emotions and thoughts and ridiculously wanton desires that pushed me to the brink. I cried out when he came, my own second sparkling explosion overwhelming. I clung to him tightly as it rolled over me, and then collapsed weakly, all of my energy gone. Michael followed not a second later, and we just lay there, naked limbs entwined atop his kitchen table.

After a time, we finally moved, with warm caresses and soft voices. Michael turned off the lights and swiftly ported us to the bedroom—*his* bedroom. We made love again, but this time it was slower and achingly sweet. While the darkness wrapped itself around us, he pressed kisses to my eyes and whispered to me that he had fallen into an endless love with me. And in the glow of his eyes, I told him that I was falling headlong in love with him, too.

There in his bed, in his arms, I fell asleep.

In the wee early hours, I woke up in Michael's bed. He didn't sleep, so I didn't expect him to be there. My assumption was that he had no reason to stay when there were other things to do. But when I turned over, he was still there—giving me a small smile and brushing a strand of hair from my face.

"Hello, stranger," I murmured, the sleep still muddling my brain.

He smiled at me, and I wrapped my arms around him, loving the feel of having him close. I kept my head tucked into his chest, enjoying the scent of him, the warmth of him. We stayed like that for a time, and I nearly fell back asleep—I was so comfortable. But eventually he pulled away.

"We need to get ready," he said.

"For what?" I asked. I was so delighted to be right where I was, and I had no desire to leave the confines of his bed.

Very seriously, he replied, "We need to track down some of Devlin's people, see how much we can find out from them."

"Track them down? Why? We're here, and they can't find us here. Can't we just stay here, protected in your magical bubble?"

"You and I both know you can't live your life from here, Celie."

I grimaced. He was right about that. But then a millisecond later, another thought occurred to me. "Hold on. Wait just one minute. If you can summon demons—nice trick by the way—then why not send them out after Devlin? Wouldn't that take care of our problem?" I was a bit perplexed that he hadn't done this before.

"I've tried that before."

Welp...

"I can't do that."

I waited for him to continue. He didn't. "So spill it already! Why not?" I exclaimed, sitting up and throwing my hands in the air. "If this is so important, tell me why!"

"It's— Well, we have rules. Doing that would break them."

"Rules? Oh great, now there are rules? What the hell, Mike?!"

I threw my hands up in the air and got out of bed. Throwing on a t-shirt he had lying on the arm of the chair, I began pacing across his room while he sat back in bed. His expression was serious, and a touch concerned. His left leg was bent, foot flat on the bed, and his arm rested on top of his knee. His dark brown hair disheveled, it hung down just past his shoulders, and I caught sight of him watching me. I glanced at him and saw he was already *ready* for me, and it was utter hell not to indulge myself with him. I unleashed a loud groan that evolved into a yell, venting my frustration.

"Demons, vampires, sons and daughters, and now rules? Goddamn rules!" I began talking to myself out loud. "This guy keeps all this shit from me—all the sordid little details of the supernatural underworld—and now that he's telling me the dirty secrets, he waits until the end of it all to let me know there are *rules*. I swear I'm gonna wring his sexy but totally maddening neck for this... I'm gonna grab it, and twist it, and then I'm gonna stomp on it..." I kept ranting and raving like an idiot, with hand gestures and everything. Then I stopped and stormed over to Michael, pointing a finger in his face. "You drive me insane!" Then I began pacing and talking to myself again.

Michael turned sheepish. "I can't send demons after another vampire—it just doesn't work that way."

Freezing in my tracks, my jaw agape, I slowly turned to stare at him. "Wow. Just—*wow*. Are you really—now, after everything that's happened—you're just *now* telling me that he's a vampire? Are you *kidding* me?"

I squinted my eyes at Michael. "Don't you think that would have been important? Hmm? Maybe somewhere in the back of your mind it was a thought that came up? 'I should probably tell Celie that Devlin—the main antagonist in our story—is a vampire.' Oh yeah, or even, 'I like you. I'm falling for you. And by the way, Devlin is a vampire, too.' Yeah, *Mike*. Either one sounds good."

Michael climbed out of bed and strode toward me—naked—with a purpose. I prepped for a fight, as he reached out and grabbed me by the shoulders, stopping me in place.

"You big ox! Let me go!" His hands were firm but gentle, and he wasn't trying to hurt me, but I hated being controlled.

"No. Not until you shut up for a minute."

"Hey, *sir*. You can't talk to me like that," I growled in warning.

"Yes, I can when you won't stop talking. I want to explain this to you, and I need you to hush." He was right in my face, a look quite stern on his face. A sense of urgency swept over me, and I knew he was being sincere and had no real intention of trying to manhandle me. He literally just wanted me to stop and hear him.

It's the same thing I would have wanted if I were in his shoes.

"Are you done?" he asked, his voice calm and quiet.

"Yes."

"Good. Now listen when I say this to you: I didn't tell you he was a vampire because I didn't want to scare you. I'm not keeping you in the dark just to be a bloody arse to you. Devlin became a vampire purely by accident. He got a sample of my DNA from that parking lot. He kept it and worked with it trying to perfect a way to turn himself. About a year ago, it finally worked."

One eyebrow raised, I wanted to be sure I correctly understood him. "So you're saying... Devlin made himself a vampire through a transfusion?"

"Basically. The problem, though, is he realized this method didn't give him the ability to turn others. Better still, all of his samples were gone. Used up through his trials."

I suddenly realized what was going on now. "He wants your blood because... Oh holy bejeezus—he wants an army, doesn't he?" Michael nodded as he removed his hands from my shoulders. "What the actual fuck, Mike?"

"Yeah, pretty much."

"Okay." I closed my eyes and took a deep breath. "Okay, okay. *Now* I understand. Now I get it."

"Good, cause we need to go."

"Go? Go where?"

He didn't answer me. "Grab some things and your sword—you were great with it. Meet me in the garage in thirty. We're taking the 300M."

"Style over protection?" I asked, puzzled at his choice.

"Who said you have to sacrifice one for the other?"

"I just thought that—ah... You have bulletproof siding, don't you?"

He arched an eyebrow at me.

I was impressed. "Nice."

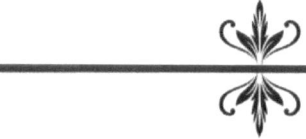

We headed out at sunset, driving around the edge of the city and into the countryside. With tangerine glow backing the trees, the forest appeared darker, blacker, and more ominous than usual. I glanced at Michael, curious if he felt the presence that seemed to reach out to me from within the trees. Without taking his eyes off the road, he nodded.

I turned back to gaze out my window. I didn't know what it was that lay out in the shadows, but I could feel it waiting for us. It was watching us, assessing us, trying to oppress us just by sheer force of will alone. It was deadly cold, dangerous, and mind-bendingly evil. I felt it trying to settle into my bones like liquid nitrogen. Burning and shivering as the ice dug deep into my veins, I cranked up the heat in the car, hoping to thaw out. Warmth flowed from the air vents, and I held my hands up to them, soaking it in like a sponge.

"Don't worry," said Michael, still focusing on the road. "It doesn't last very long."

"What is it?" I asked, my teeth practically chattering.

"Him. Raines. He's trying to seek you out. You feel his influence, his power. It's still not as powerful as my own, but then again, he was engineered, not born."

Trying to be casual, as if I was simply changing the subject, I asked, "So what, uh, what does one do to be 'born'?"

Michael arched an eyebrow, never taking his eyes from the road. "What? Are you really asking me this *now*?"

"I'm just curious, Mike. Do you need someone to just bite you? Or is there some long, drawn-out process involved?"

"Yes, a vampire bites you, and you turn." He said nothing more, remaining silent.

I waited...and waited...and waited some more. He clearly wasn't going to be forthcoming about this issue.

"Ah," I mumbled. "I see." I tapped my finger on my lower lip, deep in thought. "Well, let's say you wanted to turn someone, Mike—maybe a woman like me. Now, if you were to bite—"

"Stop!" He shouted and pulled the car off the road suddenly and violently. We skidded to a halt in the dirt and grass, and he shifted the car into park. Then he turned and leaned forward, his face angry, but I knew it was fear that gripped him. "Stop that—that thing you're trying to ask? Just stop right now! I am not going to bite you, so just get that thought out of your innocent head. It's not happening; it will *never* happen."

"But I never—"

"I don't care. Don't think it, don't wonder it, don't even *consider* the possibilities of it." He stared me down, and I withdrew in my seat a little. "I won't do it—under *any* circumstances—so just drop it."

He turned away, still trying to make me think he was angry. I watched him fall back into his seat and grip the steering wheel, knuckles turning white in an attempt to steady himself. Cautiously, I eased back up from where I had plastered myself against the passenger door.

We sat for a minute, with him staring off into space and me watching him with new eyes. Did I really know him? He told me so many things—beautiful, terrible, amazing things. Why wouldn't he tell me this? What was he protecting me from?

Before I could dive into that further, new thoughts began to emerge in my head, and they were so far away from my feelings for him. Should I be afraid of this man? Who was I to think he couldn't be dangerous in his own right? After all, he was a vampire, and he had been stalking me. I was suddenly nervous. I was with a man who I had slept with after knowing him for just a matter of weeks. Was that long enough to know him? To trust him? And to top it off, he could kill me with his bare hands or by summoning demons from Hell. He had taken me from my life and thrust me into something that was more dangerous than anything I had ever imagined. I was scared shitless of everything, and in an instant, my thoughts convinced me it was smart that I start growing scared of him.

How did I really know what the truth was? How did I get into this situation? And more importantly, how would I ever get out when the time was right? Would the time ever be right? What am I doing?

Celie... Do not fear... Come to me, and I will keep you safe...

I flinched and gasped at the intimacy of another voice in my head. Gripping the sides of my seat tightly, I thought I might dig my fingernails in and rip away the cushioning. This voice was darker, more malevolent, and seething with evil I had never felt with Michael.

And this voice was in my head.

Michael snapped upright. He reached over and turned my face to him, slowly, like we were both underwater. He looked deep into my eyes, his own glowing silver in the darkness.

All I could do was stare back and say, "He's inside of me."

"Are you sure?" he whispered, concern etched in all of his features.

I can protect you, Celie... Come to me... Come...

I felt fingertips stroking me along my spine—but from *within*. "Oh God, Mike... He, he's planting fears—" Pain gripped me and I seized up for a moment, gritting my teeth. "He's— I'm fighting to— Devlin— He's trying to—" I was intensely frigid—and scared—and on the verge of passing out. I felt the fingers reaching past my ribcage, trying to locate my heart. The feeling of being touched from the inside was the most revolting and appalling violation I could ever know. Then he pinched a nerve, and I jerked, ready to scream at the horrifying control Devlin had.

Michael's gaze narrowed as his brow knit together. "What?" I stiffened from the sensations and shook my head. He persisted. "What is he trying to do?" His touch was gentle, stroking my temples, his breath warm against my cheek. His voice was also stern, trying to get me to focus.

The contact from Devlin left me completely despondent. And to have to admit what I had been feeling... I couldn't bear to look at Michael, so I closed my eyes. My jaw clenched tight as the sensations permeated my body, I whispered, "He wants—" I shuddered. "He wants me to fear you."

He doesn't love you... I can hide you from him... Come...

I heard Michael stop breathing. Then both of his hands were on my cheeks again, and I felt him lean forward. He placed his lips to my forehead and then touched his own to mine. "I would never hurt you, Celie. If anything, you bloody scared me! I thought you were asking me— I thought that you wanted me to—"

When he pulled back, I opened my eyes, and his words faltered, his voice falling away.

"I love you," he said softly, "and I don't want you to become a monster—like me, like I am right now, like Raines made himself to be. I never meant to upset you. Seeing you safe and alive—that's all I want, all I ever wanted." He leaned forward again, touched his forehead to mine, and held us together.

I began to breathe easier and realized the voice was gone. My body was back under my control. "It stopped," I murmured.

Michael pulled back and tried a small smile. "We can fight him as long as we're together. This is how we'll win. Just have faith in me, in yourself—have faith in *us*. He can't win this: he'll never win. You'll see. All of this will work out in time."

"Will it?" I asked tentatively. Tears rose up behind my eyes, and I fought them back. "Will it ever be okay?" I couldn't live like this, with terrifying creatures chasing me and madmen trying to claim me. I especially couldn't live like this if I couldn't trust the man who had told me he loved me and would protect me.

Reading my thoughts and emotions, Michael took hold of my hands, his face solemn. "You can trust me. I would never do anything to hurt you or chase you from my life." He spoke earnestly. "Listen to what's inside you, inside your heart. You know we are meant to be."

I looked at him for a moment, felt our hands together, his thumb rubbing across the back of my knuckles. The silence in my head told me Michael was giving me space. I could hear my heartbeat, and my own voice—mine—spoke to me from within. It told me that I wasn't just falling in love with Michael—I already had. But the strangeness of everything, the surprises and scares, the prospect of what was to come: it was all overwhelming me. I was drowning in its frightening bizarreness, and I couldn't breathe. My thoughts and feelings had been laid out in a giant mess, and I was struggling to put the pieces back together.

Laying my head back on the seat, I stared at the roof above my head. "I want to trust you—I do." I sighed the sigh of the truly weary. "I just need some time to wrap my head around this. It's all been so, so crazy, and things just keep happening... These are things that— You know, I'm getting thrown curveballs like I've never seen in my *life*. How am I supposed to feel normal again?" I looked down and met his gaze. "It's really hard to *deal* with all of this—to process it."

"I'll give you time. I'll give you anything you need. If it takes me your entire life to earn your trust, it will be time well spent."

"Why are you so amazing?"

"'Cause I have you." He gave him his most charismatic smile. "Are you ready to keep going?"

"Maybe we could wait here for a little bit?" I think just knowing he was willing to give me time made him more attractive, and I couldn't help the thoughts in my head—or the words that came out of my mouth. "While we wait, I'm sure we can find something to occupy our time..." I waggled my eyebrows at him.

"Is that so? Would you like to drive, or do you prefer to ride?"

I laughed. "Oh god, Mike. That's so awful, I can't help but love it." I laughed again. "You're too damn sexy for your own good."

He laughed, too, and then he kissed me, his hands holding my head and his lips warm against mine. In seconds, we were breathless and escaped to the backseat. I knew he was dangerous for me, but I didn't care. I still wasn't sure if my fears were legitimate or just the product of *him*, that stupid, vile voice that had been in my head. The only person that is truly trustworthy shows you they can be trusted, but the fact that Michael was willing to spend my entire life earning my trust was definitely saying a lot.

I knew then I would never love anyone the way I loved him.

Chapter Five

They Happen to Have Teeth

On the road once more, we headed further and further into the night. I didn't feel the presence again, but that didn't prevent me from being tense as hell waiting for it. After an hour or so, Michael turned the car into the parking lot of a rundown church Everything was overgrown and dilapidated. The pond water was stagnant, and the parking lot was weed ridden. Any trees on the property were dead or dying. The white paint of the exterior church walls was peeling and had come off the steeple and most of the front walls. Up above, the roof was sunken in and rotten, with patches of shingles missing from various spots.

I read the sign as we drove up: Blessed Light of Our Holy Mother. It was a Catholic Church I recalled having attended once or twice with a friend's family—as a child, though. Several years ago, I heard it had closed down—something to do with allegations against the clergy. I hadn't been surprised to hear it, of course. I remembered how my friend hadn't wanted to go to church that second Sunday. She had kicked and screamed to keep from going to the counseling session with the priest, but her parents demanded it because of her school troubles. In my mind, I could still see how she looked when she left his office: her mussed hair, her twisted dress, her tear-stained cheeks...

Michael pulled up near the back door, put on the brake, and turned off the engine. "Here we are," he said as he climbed out. I looked at him in confusion and then climbed out my side.

"Here we are *where*?"

"We need to get a few things."

"In a church?"

Michael looked over his shoulder and smiled at me. Before I realized what was going on, he had reached the back door, took hold of the chains keeping the doors locked, and tore them apart like they were nothing.

I placed a hand on his shoulder. "You can't just go breaking into churches. Is this some weird hobby you've got? Or—wait—do we need holy water?"

He chuckled softly. "No, I store a few things here." At my quizzical gaze, he added, "For safekeeping."

"You store things in a *church*? You know that they make these things called 'storage units' that you can rent, right?"

Michael just smirked at me.

"Well, aren't you afraid they'll tear this place down? I'm sure the owners have other plans for it."

"I don't think so."

"Why? Do you know them or something?"

Yanking open the doors, he met my stare. "*I'm* the owner." Then he disappeared inside.

I followed him into the dark where everything was pitch black. Sliding my feet across the floor, I wanted to tread carefully and avoid bumping into anything. Ahead of me, I heard Michael mumble, 'Aziz—light!' and there it was. Light flooded the space, and I saw Michael was handing me a flashlight. He crossed the main floor past the pews, and through a doorway. From there, we proceeded down into the depths of the building.

I had no idea where I was going, but he did, and it was directly to a door at the back of the main office. Opening it wide, I peeked around him and saw a staircase that wound down in a spiral toward the cellar. Michael held his hand out to say 'after you,' and so I went, feeling my way down the stone lining the walls. We reached the bottom, and I froze.

Across from the small dirt floor at the bottom of the staircase was another door—tall and made from sturdy wood planks. It wasn't that I was scared of light or seeing a door there. It was nothing of the kind. What scared me was that I heard voices coming from the other side of that door, with light shining from underneath it. Who was that? I turned back to ask Michael if he was expecting anyone.

His expression was surprising.

Michael was staring at the door, a look of absolute fury on his face. I knew then that he had no idea someone would be here. I also knew that whoever was on the other side of that door was going to get a serious ass-whooping. He motioned for me to be silent and closed his eyes.

I stood there, a bit puzzled, wondering what he was doing for a minute. Then I realized it must be something with his abilities. After some time had passed, I started getting impatient. I was tempted to start tapping my foot, but no one likes a pissed-off vampire. Clamping my arms down to my sides, I began counting to ten. When I got to eight, he opened his eyes.

Two Sons, and they sound a bit on the slow side, he thought to me.

I snorted. *I thought that was a given. What are they doing in there?*

Planning on coming after us—well, you, *namely. Sounds like they're trying to get in good with their boss by grabbing you on their own.*

Lovely. I smirked at him. *Go out for milk and bring back a present, eh?* He just shrugged. *What a bunch of lap dogs...*

That's true, but in this case, they happen to have teeth. They both have semi-autos in there, and I think one of them was carrying a grenade.

Jesus, Mike—a grenade? Who do they think they are?

I'm sure you'll be fine. Should be easy for you after the two demons at the house.

Easy for you to say. These two have guns, and I'm not bulletproof like the car.

But they're just human. The other two were demons—as in, ascended from Hell?

I'd really *appreciate it if you didn't bring them up again, okay? Really, I would. Thanks.*

Michael reached over and mussed my hair, causing me to crinkle my nose like an annoyed child. I smacked his arm away.

You wanna go in? I gestured with both hands that this time, he should be the one to go first. In response, he simply smiled, and his sharp teeth gleamed in the dimly lit stairwell. *Then let's do this.*

Leaning back slightly, he kicked open the door.

It was a wine cellar-slash-survivalist depot. Some communion wine was still stored here, as well as a bunch of supplies Michael had accumulated over time. There were guns, knives, bundles of rope, gas canisters, food stores, water, gasoline, clothing, and tons of other items that I couldn't even identify. A wooden work bench was on either side of the ten by twenty-foot room, with barrels full of silver bullets lining the back wall between them.

In front of the bench on the left stood the two Sons, burlap sacks in their hands. One was tall, lanky, and extremely sickly in appearance. His sallow skin was stark against the black clothing he wore. His mouse brown hair was practically pasted across his forehead, and on his face was a disdainful expression, as if a permanent sneer was affixed to him. The other was of average height, with a slight build and longer, wavy brown hair parted in the middle. He wore glasses and had a ruddy complexion, leaving me to think he might have had a few drinks before this adventure they were undertaking. Perhaps he had needed to build up his courage to go.

Slow was really an inadequate description for both of them. When we burst into the room, all they did was look up at us. No one moved, no one breathed. It would be easier to say they acted like they had the mental equivalent of chimps that had been smoking pot all day.

"Hello boys!" I said cheerily. "Fancy seeing you here!" I was trying to sound positive despite the nervousness I felt with the amount of firepower they had on that work bench: it was covered in guns of all sizes and makes. I recognized two of the gun brands, but that was it, and it was enough.

"Wot...wot are you doin' 'ere?" said the tall one, his cockney accent heavy and thick. His eyes narrowed as he took in both of us. "Boss said you two would be away..." He exchanged glances with his partner.

"Did he now?" Michael was all too calm, and even I knew that meant trouble. He casually walked to the right and began toying with a bit of rope lying on the opposite workbench. "Seems your boss has been saying a lot of things about me that aren't true."

I caught the short Son staring at me intently. "What?" I barked at him. He jumped slightly and bumped into a barrel.

"Are you Cecelia Moore?" asked Tall one, peering at me intently with squinty eyes. When I didn't answer, he turned to Michael. "That yer girl, mate?"

"Yeah, she's mine."

I glanced at Michael, both flattered that he thought of me that way and also annoyed that I was being referred to like a toy. I stood my ground, though, ready for anything but getting really pissed off.

"Glad you brought her 'ere." To me, he said, "Me and Rodger was gonna come lookin' for you two in a minute."

Michael looked at him and smiled slyly. "Oh, you were, huh? Whatever for...?"

This time, Rodger spoke, excited by finding out who I was. "We're taking her back with us!" His expression was greedy, like I was a prize.

I stopped that thought right there. "No, no, no. I don't think so. You two—" I pointed back and forth between both Sons, "—are not taking *me* anywhere."

"Yes, we are," replied Rodger and he stepped forward.

"Bullshit, honky boy. No you're not." I took my own step forward and kicked him square in the balls. He doubled over and grabbed himself. The Tall one just stood there, gaping like he had seen a donkey fly. I don't know—maybe he had? Then he turned and came after me, both determined and angry.

I dodged to the right as he dove for me, bumping into Michael. Michael grabbed me from behind by both arms and moved me to the side. Bending down, he picked up the Tall one from where he'd fallen to the floor, grabbing him just under his jaw. His hand wrapped around Tall Guy's throat, Michael held him up in the air and slammed him into the stone wall.

"You really shouldn't be doing things like that," he muttered angrily. Turning to me, he thought, *Get Devlin's location from the other one on the floor.*

Don't you know where he is?

He moves the cult every three or four weeks. I haven't found the new location, yet.

Okay, I'll get it. I winked and blew him a kiss.

"That bitch deserves a good smack," said the Tall one, and I glared at him. He looked over and sneered at me. "Lemme go, and I'll wallop 'er a good one."

I heard his voice squeak as Michael tightened his grip. "Yeah, well that's not gonna happen," I called to him as I walked over to miserable Rodger. He was still lying on the dirt floor, curled up in the fetal position. With both of them out of commission, I was feeling much braver, bolder. I stepped across him with one leg and crouched down over top of him. Rolling him over, I held him by the chin.

"Now Rodger, I need you to tell me where your 'Boss' is."

Rodger just stared at me and kept silent.

"Don't tell 'er nothing, Rodge!"

Rodger looked over at him, his eyes pleading for help.

"Keep yer trap—" The Tall one's voice was silenced from his perch, and a low growl escaped Micheal's throat. I could just imagine the look on his face as he stared into the eyes of that lanky creep.

"Don't look at him," I said, jerking his face back to look at me. "I'm the one you need to worry about." Rodger stared at me worriedly, but I just smiled sweetly down at him. After a minute of saying nothing, I pulled out my sword and placed it at his throat. He swallowed but still remained silent. That hocked me off, so I hauled my arm back to punch him.

He cried out, "Okay! Please! Just don't—don't hurt me, okay?"

"Damn it! You bloody fucking *sissy*!" shouted Tall Guy, and then he gagged, choking as Michael's vise-like grip contracted.

I continued to hold my blade at his neck. "So? Talk to me, buddy."

"He's—" Rodger's eyes darted to the Tall one, "He's on the outskirts."

"Of Bantum?"

He nodded before singing like a canary. "There's an abandoned warehouse at the edge of the business park—Porter Range Industrial. Everyone's in there." He looked up into my eyes. "He wants you." Then he looked at Michael. "*Both* of you. And he's not going to stop until he does."

Slightly unnerved, I patted his cheek. "Good job, bud, but he's not getting anybody."

Michael leaned in and spoke quietly—menacingly—to the Tall Son. His voice was so quiet I could barely hear him, and when I did, it was ice cold.

"Here me now, Son. You two are going to go back to your 'Boss'. You're going to tell him that *we're* coming for *him*." He squeezed the guy's neck like a python and turned the man's head, speaking low into his ear. "You're going to give him something from me, too." Pulling out a folded piece of paper, he slid it into the breast pocket of the Tall one's shirt. Patting it roughly, he added, "Tell him to remember." Even lower still, he whispered, "If he so much as touches a hair on her head, I *will* kill him. And I've killed dozens of people of far greater importance."

Then Michael gnashed his teeth together just a hair's breadth away from the guy's ear, causing him to flinch. With a sound of disgust, Michael hauled the Tall one back and tossed him out of the room. He landed onto the first of the stone steps with a thud, and I know I heard something break upon landing. I also let go of my prey, standing up to step back from Rodger. He scrambled to his feet and ran, collecting his friend before they rushed up the stairs like they were on fire. The door at the top of the stairwell slammed shut behind them.

"So..." I exhaled and focused on slowing down the outrageous beat of my heart. "That was...interesting."

"You okay?" He sounded concerned, but he was also still staring at the staircase.

"Yeah, sure. I don't think I've ever kicked a guy so hard in my entire life," I said, laughing.

Michael grimaced and turned to me. "I felt that one, you know. OUCH. Remind me not to piss you off."

I saluted him. "Will do."

Scanning the room, I inquired, "So what were we getting from in here? You obviously had some ideas before we were interrupted." Then I remembered that weird bit moments ago. "Oh, and by the way—why in God's name did you tell them to let Devlin know we're coming? Isn't that what they call a 'dead giveaway'? Pun *definitely* intended."

"No. If he can use his powers like earlier, then he already knows. I just wanted those two scared shitless. And yes, we need to go ahead and get some things. We'll start with those." Michael pointed to the guns the Sons left on the bench. "Let's get moving."

I kept my mouth shut. Something was still off. What was that piece of paper? I tucked that into the back of my brain for safe keeping: I would absolutely be bringing that up later.

We grabbed a few of the gas canisters (tear gas), gas masks, and a case of silver bullets. Once that was loaded into the car, we came back for more guns from the shelves, water, M.R.E.'s (Meal Ready to Eat), and handcuffs. (Actually, I grabbed two of those—one for now and one for later, if you know what I mean.) I also picked up a crucifix or two, but Michael reminded me they don't work.

Specifically, he asked," Do you really think that Bram Stoker got it *all* right?"

Needless to say, I put them back. We shoved the last bit into some military-issue duffle bags that he had higher up on a shelf.

As we left the room, Michael decided that he couldn't leave everything lying around for the Sons and Daughters to come back for. He took some gasoline and poured it around the room, trailing it behind us as we went back up the stairs. After loading the final bags into the car, he pulled out a matchbook, then he lit one and tossed it towards the church. The flames consumed the old wood in seconds, and we both turned and got into the car.

As he drove away, I turned around in my seat, watching the fire grow smaller and smaller behind us. Seconds later, the explosion hit. I jumped, instinctively ducking down in my seat as the church flew apart into thousands of pieces. Smoke and embers rose high into the sky like a beautiful orange flower blooming in the night. Debris pelted the roof of the car. I peeked over my seat and watched as the building was devoured, the remainder of the roof and walls caving in and smothering the basement.

"Where to now?" I asked, continuing to gaze at the remnants.

"Now, we go to the industrial park."

"We're going straight over to get him?" I exclaimed, incredulous that we'd just head right there, immediately after dispatching his Sons to 'warn' him.

"No. I thought we could spend a night at my shop." Michael turned to look at me. "You need to rest."

"Rest. Right. I could do that." I gave him a secretive smile. See, I actually had other plans in mind.

We got to his shop roughly forty-five minutes later. It was tucked away in a little Bohemian part of the city that was rapidly gentrifying. The front face of the building was brick, with an art deco style that was evident in the doorway and window designs. Trees lined the sidewalk out front and went down the street. The iron wrought streetlamps glowed softly with flickering bulbs intended to imitate candles. It was altogether peaceful and reminiscent of a time gone by, and all I could seem to think of was Michael's assistant, Ginny. She must have loved working here.

Damn that bastard...

Michael parked his Chrysler two blocks down and on a side street. We walked to his shop but didn't go in the front door—too obvious! He headed around the corner and pulled down the fire escape. Michael went up first, easily lifting me up, and we climbed to the third floor. He purposely broke a window for us to get inside, and once we were in, we got settled. While I explored his collections on the first floor, he set up a cozy area for us towards the back of the third.

I came back after some time to find him relaxing, sitting in an old 1940s swivel chair, like you would find at a detective's desk in a police station or some noir novel. He had a nice cold beer in his left hand. His grey t-shirt was smudged but clung to his muscular biceps and shoulders. His black jeans were dusty on his legs, but they failed to hide the outline of his cock between his thighs. Seeing him sitting there, with his strong legs spread wide, elbows resting on the arms of the chair, and a thick section of hair grazing the side of his face, nothing was sexier to me. His silver eyes seemed to glow as they met mine.

"Comfortable?" I asked, amused to see him in such a casual, non-dramatic state. It was refreshing and reminded me he was still a man and not just a vampire. I didn't get to see much of him that way.

"It's almost like home," he said and smiled. I smiled back, happy to see him so settled. I knew this place held some bad memories for him, but I also knew it held a lot of good ones, too.

"So now what? We just wait?"

"Yeah. Wait until morning. Then we'll go to Porter Range and find that warehouse. We need to surveil it, find out the defenses." He took another drink from his bottle. "The last thing we want is to go in there without knowing all of the exits." He winked. "Just in case."

Across the walkway from him, I sat down on a travel trunk. "Don't you think the cops might help? I mean, it would be a whole hell of a lot easier for them to arrest him, right? Or the FBI? Report him as running a cult with guns, and it's guaranteed they'd be interested in that. They'd bring him down, and we'd be done."

"But there's no guarantee that they would bring in all of his followers. And if he's still alive, they would still do what he wants, executing any plans he already has set in motion. He could order them around from jail, even if he's in solitary."

I leaned back on my elbows. "That answers that, then." I sighed. "Now I get why he's gotta die."

"Yes."

We sat in silence for a while. Then something from the church that had been nagging at me caught up to us. "Hey, when you said Bram Stoker didn't get it all right back there, and we talked about some of this before, but I still don't have a full picture of what you can do...?"

Michael leaned forward and set down his now empty beer. Leaning back into the chair, he propped his feet up on the desk nearby and clasped his hands behind his head. "Bram Stoker... Boy, that guy had an imagination." He laughed and started telling me about all the other myths and legends that were exactly that—and some that weren't.

Michael told me about the real vampire history, including which parts were real and which were not. He told me about Lilith, the first wife of Adam (you know, before Eve?), who had left him because of his obsessive need for control. She was inaccurately dubbed the vampire queen in ancient texts because of her insubordination and unwillingness to succumb and be dominated. Literally, it was an attempt to discredit her. She was the first woman to empower herself and walk away from an unhappy union, so why wouldn't the men of that time want to keep her under their boot?

There were also various versions of vampires indicated in various Roman and Greek mythology called Lamiae, Empusae, and Striges. They were goddesses who would take on human form to seduce their victims in order to drink their blood—not unlike what some people refer to as a succubus or succubi. During the same time frame, when Christianity was winning the battle against pagan rituals, the Holy Communion wound up instigating vampirism. Some people confused their original pagan beliefs with the actual presence of Jesus's flesh and blood during the act of communion, and they took to cannibalism and drinking real human blood. Everyone from Aztecs to Eskimos had stories of vampirism.

Then, in the 14th Century, the bubonic plague killed thousands of people, and vampires were blamed. Of course, Michael told me this wasn't true. He told me that, in a panic and fearful of catching the disease, people would bury others without verifying that they were really dead. Those that were buried alive would claw out of their graves and be found covered in blood from their own wounds. Naturally, they were called vampires for having 'risen from the grave'.

One hundred years later, two famous characters were labeled with the curse. One was Gilles de Rais, a Frenchman who murdered hundreds of children in his experiments to discover the secret of the

Philosopher's Stone. The other was Dracula, also known as Vlad Tepes Dracula, the Prince of Wallachia (Romania). When battling the Ottomans, he would impale those he killed on tall spikes, drinking their blood in celebration of his victories.

The year 1611 brought us the Blood Countess, Elizabeth Bathory. She thought drinking and bathing in the blood of young virgin girls would keep her young. She kidnapped and tortured many before she was discovered and locked away in a tower for the rest of her life. Her story was the last time anyone really spoke of vampire-style activity.

"The rest was superstitious nonsense and folklore. Actually, there was an outbreak of rabies around 1720 that people thought were vampires. Rabies looks a lot like it when compared to the myths: people reacting violently to light and mirrors, baring their teeth, frothing at the mouth, trying to bite people, etc..

"I also heard stories from the sailors at the docks. They talked about towns in Europe where they sent virgins (boys and girls) out on virgin horses to run through cemeteries at night. Townspeople would drive nails through the foreheads of the corpses they thought were vampires. I didn't believe any of it..." Michael stood up and grabbed another beer, shrugging. "After Amelia, though..." He paused, a memory digging at him, and then he downed some of his beverage. "Well, it all came together after her."

I was leaning forward now, totally enthralled. "What about...um...I think a disease where light hurts? Oh, damnit, I can never remember the name of it! It starts with a 'p' or something? Por, porf, porif—"

"Porphyria?"

"Yes! The one with the pale skin and whatnot?"

"Yeah, it looks the same but people with that don't actually drink blood."

I hung my head down. "Right. Of course." I realized what time it was and my head popped back up. "Speaking of that—isn't it time for you to...?" I let my voice trail off.

He nodded. "You're right. You never know what tomorrow is going to bring." Michael got up from his chair and started to walk past me.

At the last minute, I grabbed his arm, a desire for something overcoming me so much, I just had to have it—I had to have *him*. He stopped and looked down at me. I slid the handcuffs out from where I'd had them nestled in my back pocket, watching as they dangled from my hand between us.

"You're right, Michael." My chin still tilted down, I looked up at him with doe eyes and a bat of my eyelashes. "You never know what tomorrow is going to bring—or tonight." I gave a pout of my lips, and he took the bait.

He urgently pulled me toward him, wrapping his arms around me, and kissed me so passionately—so ferociously—that I knew he had been feeling it, too. I swear I forgot what year it was—forgot my own damn name—it was so intense. An overwhelming, overpowering magnetism surged within me, and his was the only direction I could go. I wasn't just his—he was *mine*. I needed to have him—and in every possible way. I let him rip off my clothes, not caring if they ripped—*loving* that they ripped. He held me like I was his lifeline, and when I felt that rumble in his chest, when I heard that growl emanate from his throat, I nearly collapsed at the sound. At that moment, he was all I wanted.

This one day of intense, adrenaline-fueled escapades had my body craving him, yearning for him. I was even more aroused knowing he was craving me with the same intensity. It was insane that we felt this way about each other, but it was real, and neither of us could deny it.

He laid me onto the floor, gently placing me down before we became nothing but a tangle of naked limbs entwined in ardor and passion. He used the handcuffs and hooked me to a broken radiator pipe. From there, it was ecstasy. He focused solely on driving me to the brink with nothing but his teeth and tongue. Michael teased me and tempted me, flicking his tongue over my clit and nibbling on the inside of my thigh. His fingers pinched and rolled my nipples, and I called out his name as he brought me to the edge over and over again. I arched against his mouth, feeling wild with need as he tortured me. Every touch of his fingers, I tried to get him to push them inside me, but he refused. Every stroke of his tongue, I tried to ride him, but he denied me. I began to whimper, desperation leaving me wanton. As if a madness had claimed him, he spread my legs apart and put one up over his shoulder. Gently at first, he eased inside of me, and I nearly buckled at the sensation. In seconds, he began thrusting, driving himself into me—faster and faster, harder and harder. I begged him to release me, and he growled again, ready to do as I asked. As I clutched the handcuffs, he took us both higher, rising up to burn us both in furious flames. I nearly screamed from the carnal pleasure.

Then I felt it—an animal urge, a desire to have him truly take me as only he could. His head near my face, I leaned forward and moaned in his ear, "Do it. Take all of me." When he looked up at my face, I knew what I was thinking was written all over it. I thought I was being seductive and bold, opening my thoughts up to him to make sure he was fully aware of my intentions.

He froze, a quiet stillness taking hold of him, and I felt him pull back from me in every way. Suddenly, I was very cold and alone. He had retreated from me fully. In an instant, I knew I had fucked up: I had pushed him in a way I shouldn't have. I felt exposed and vulnerable, and I was still handcuffed.

Michael leaned over me and used the key to unlock the cuffs. He leaned back and stared down at my face while I brought down my arms, rubbing one of my wrists. His eyes were sorrowful, his expression torn. He pulled a blanket over me and grabbed his clothes.

"No, Celie," he whispered. "I can't— I just can't..."

Then he stood up and left me there, ashamed of myself beneath a blanket on the cold floor.

He got his 'drink' somewhere else.

Chapter Six

CONFIDENTIAL

Morning was bright, sunny, and totally depressing. I had totally screwed up the previous night. I'm not sure what I had been thinking, asking him for something like that. Apparently, I was a moron—first class, give me a medal. I was a grade A, number one, worldly idiot. Now I felt like the entire population of Earth was aware of my stupidity and utter shamelessness. I wanted to crawl into a hole and die a ridiculously painful death—one that only number one idiots were deserving of.

Michael had already told me that he didn't want to bite me. He'd made that loud and clear. He had even gone as far as to tell me not to think about it—thoughts were dangerous. When he had gotten so incredibly angry about it the other day, I hadn't really been asking him. I had just been curious—thinking. But being with him last night, being close to him, I felt a need somewhere inside of me. It felt right, damn it! I couldn't just ignore it, or else I would have been lying to myself.

And now...

Lord help me, but now I knew it was going to have to happen. When he walked away from me, I thought about reasons why it might have felt so right. I knew I couldn't spend the rest of my life growing old and watching him stay young. At some point I would die, and he would keep going. I'd seen that movie, and I just couldn't fathom winding up debilitated or diseased and having him trying to cuddle up with me. The thought of any of it just made me want to throw up. I couldn't avoid the thoughts, the visions of me dying and him wandering the earth alone again.

That cemented it: I was in love with him.

I had no words to describe how much I felt it driving me. It was utterly consuming me, and I knew that the only way I could really be with him would be if he turned me. It wasn't about personal gain, or power, or revenge. No one ever truly benefited from being turned, according to the movies—there were too many cons and not enough pros. At the same time, I had one really big pro—love. I just needed him, needed to be with him, and I had to let him know.

As I lay there, I had more and more thoughts consume me. Was I obsessed? Was I totally sure he felt the same way about me? Self-doubt was always a killer for a relationship, and I had it in spades. I wanted to be strong, but he made me feel weak in the knees. I wanted to be a powerhouse of feminine energy, and he left me wondering how I could possibly live in a world without him. Was this real? Or was this all just a dream I hadn't woken up from?

Finding him and telling him was my first priority. When he had left me, I had curled my naked body up in the bed he had made for us—*us*. But I was in that bed alone—*alone*. Worse still, when I woke up he still wasn't there. A hollow pit started yawning open inside of me. I hated not knowing where he was, and that I was alone without him. *Was he just gone? Or did he leave me?* Until I found him and told him I was head-over-heels in love with him, nothing would be right.

I wouldn't be right.

Grabbing one of the blankets, I wrapped myself up in it like a nomadic tribe woman, all hooded and cloaked. I winced at the sunshine coming through the windows. If there were any Care Bears out there, they could all kiss my ass today; it was too bright out.

Traipsing down the stairs to the second floor, there was still no sign of him. I swung around the railing and headed towards the back. I found a telephone—a rotary dial, ancient and orange. I realized I hadn't spoken to Kat in a hot minute, so I decided to use that opportunity to call her before I did anything else.

"Hey sweetie, were you worried?"

"Oh my god, Celie! Are you kidding? It's been almost three weeks! Your boss has been going crazy looking for you!"

"Sorry. Can you call them again for me? Tell them I had to take care of a relative or something?"

"Sure, you know I can. But where the hell are you? Guam? You can't pick up the phone on the regular to call me?"

I laughed and sat down on a nearby bar stool, still wrapped up in the blanket. "No, I didn't go to Guam. If I had, I'd be a hell of a lot tanner." I paused to examine one of my legs, noticing that—in addition to still being super pale—I was overdue for a shave.

But of course, I thought.

"I'm actually in—" I stopped myself. I loved Kat—she was like a sister to me—but I wasn't sure if I should tell her where I was, just in case someone was listening in.

Wow. Was I getting paranoid? Or was I getting paranoid?

"Celie?"

"Yeah, sorry. I'm in Vegas. Kind of a spur-of-the-moment thing."

"Vegas? Seriously?"

"Yup. Just kind of happened."

"And you couldn't ask me to go with you?"

"Sorry, hon. I just felt my luck pulling at me to bet on black, so I ran with it."

"Mmm hmm. Did you win anything? Are you coming back as a kajillionaire?"

"I think I just broke even."

"Dang," she muttered. I knew she wasn't convinced, but I just couldn't tell her the truth. Not yet, anyway. "Well, I'm glad you're okay. But next time you better call me earlier than this and tell me where the hell you went!" I couldn't blame her for being angry.

I nodded, even though she couldn't see me. "I promise. But listen, I've gotta go."

"What? You *just* called me!"

"I know, and I'm sorry, but I have a salon appointment on the strip, so I've gotta go. Love ya! Bye!" I hung up quickly to avoid an argument. More time talking meant more lies, and I felt horrible lying to her. Hanging up seemed like the best idea.

"Vegas, huh? Nice choice."

I spun around and there was a really attractive man standing at the top of the landing. He looked to be about Michael's age (or the age he was when he died, anyway), with rich, dark brown skin and light golden eyes. His head was clean-shaven: his face bare except for a goatee. There was a slight accent in his deep, velvety voice that I couldn't place. And boy, did I mention he was attractive? His tight charcoal shirt clearly showed muscles that were purrrrr-fect.

"What the—are you *all* male models?"

"Sorry?"

"Thanks? No offense, but who the hell are you, hot stuff?"

"I could ask you the same question," he replied, arching an eyebrow at me.

"Fair enough. I'm Celie," I said, pointing to myself before pointing at him. "Your turn."

"Name's Xander. Xander Williams." He came down the steps and reached out, and I stood up to cautiously shake his hand. I didn't know who this guy was, and I wasn't about to let my guard down now.

Backing up, I sat back down on the bar stool, careful to maintain my blanket's strategic placement. After all, I didn't have a single shred of clothing underneath it.

He looked me up and down. "Michael asked me to come and watch the place while he's out. What'd he ask you to do?"

"'Scuse me?" I retorted sharply. His insinuation—no matter how accurate it might be—was offensive.

"Nothing."

"Mmm hmm..." I watched him closely. "You said you talked to him?"

"Yeah, he said he had some business to take care of at the industrial park. Something about checking up on an old acquaintance."

"Ah..." I kept my expression calm but inside I was fuming. He'd gone to check out the place without me! Great—I hated being left out of the loop. "Did he say when he'd be back?"

"Nah, but I'm sure if he gets hung up, he'll call."

"Oh, okay." In a tit-for-tat move, I gave Xander a once-over, top to bottom, and then back up again. "And how do you know Michael?"

Xander gave a small grin. "I work for him. Some days I'm unloading the shipments that come into the shop. Other days, he sends me out to get new items. I go to places like estate sales, foreign markets, auction houses, et cetera. I buy 'em and bring 'em in." Jerking his thumb back at himself, he added, "I'm the go-to guy around here."

"Must be fun to work with a friend. Been to a lot of foreign countries?"

"Most of 'em. Can't say I liked Portugal all that much." He made a face. "Too dry."

"So then how do you know about Vegas if you don't like dry places?"

"Didn't say I don't like high rollin'. I just don't like *dry*."

I laughed and decided that Xander might be all right. "You got a girlfriend?"

He crossed his arms over his chest and looked at me questioningly. "Why? You hittin' on me, lady?"

"*No*. But I have a friend who I think you might find really interesting."

"I'm always up for meeting new people." He smiled, and it was a touch more genuine. "So you tell me: have you known Michael long?"

"Um, that depends on perspective." *Tread carefully*, I told myself.

"Okay..." said Xander, stretching out the word, sounding a bit perplexed and almost begging for an explanation.

I shrugged and just said, "It's a long story."

"Gotcha."

"What about you?"

"Probably twelve years now," he replied.

"Really? That is a long time..."

"Yeah, I met him in college. Been friends ever since."

"So he *did* go to college," I mumbled to myself.

"What was that?"

"Oh, nothing. Please continue."

"Not much more to tell. We're just great friends!" Xander laughed, then looked concerned. "Well listen, I, uh, need to go back and do some more inventory. I'll leave you up here to, uh, get dressed? Yeah?" I blushed. "Will you be alright, if I leave you here? I'll be right downstairs if you need anything." I nodded. "Great. Um, if you need me, just call me." He gave a quick smile, then turned and headed back down to the first floor, the stairs creaking beneath his feet.

I looked around the second floor and sighed. *Damn it, Mike—why do you have to do everything on your own?* Heading back upstairs, I washed up in the third-floor bathroom. After throwing on some clean jeans and a midnight blue t-shirt, I started exploring again. I found some older literature, original copies of Charles Dickens and Oscar Wilde. There was also an original copy of Carmilla by Sheridan Le Fanu and—oh my word—one of Bram Stoker's Dracula. Seeing both of them made me giggle. I would never let Michael live down having *those* in his library.

I wandered back down to the second floor and found Michael's desk, which had piles of papers strewn across it. I wasn't prone to snooping, but something caught my attention. It was from the Genaro Regional Hospital, dated about three weeks ago. I would've passed it by, but I was born there, and clearly he was not. *What's he doing communicating with the hospital?* I knew he had an arrangement to get 'transfusions', but this letter wasn't about that.

I read the letter and gasped: the letter was about *me*.

Michael had written to the hospital to get a copy of my birth certificate. It didn't make any sense. Why would he need to see a birth certificate, let alone *my* birth certificate? I read further into the letter, and they stated they were sending him a copy, to be received in two week's time.

That would've been a week ago...

I started rifling through the papers looking for it. I found a gold-colored, letter-sized envelope marked 'CONFIDENTIAL' about halfway through the pile. I took it and reached across the desk to grab a letter opener.

Ripping across the edge of the envelope, I withdrew the certificate inside. I knew what it would say: born October 13, 1989, mother Anne Moore, father Timothy Blair, etc. But obviously Michael was looking for something in particular. I wrenched it out of the envelope and flattened it down on the desk, quickly scanning through the writing. Then I saw something different, and I nearly passed out.

No... Oh, Holy Christ...

According to the certificate, Timothy Blair wasn't my father. The man who left my mother and me when I was five years old, the man who I spent my entire life despising for being a deadbeat... The same man who had a new family, with other children, and never even once attempted to contact me... This man was not who had given me half of my DNA. No, the man who really was my father was probably the most vile man to ever come into my life.

Devlin Raines.

I fell down to the floor in a heap, stunned, paralyzed by news that the man who wanted to use me and kill me to get to Michael was my *real* father. I didn't know what to do. I couldn't think; I couldn't even breathe. My heart was pounding, my chest tightening. If I was having a heart attack, I couldn't have gotten up the energy to call out or get to the phone. I felt like someone had cut my legs out from under me. I was outraged and bewildered, and I was simultaneously devastated.

Without looking, I reached up and haphazardly pulled the certificate off the desk. A few other papers fell down to the floor as I brought the document down in front of me to read it all over again, falling like razor-sharp snowflakes. My eyes scanned the words once more, analyzing it letter by letter through my gradually blurring vision.

My father...

This couldn't be possible. My mother had never mentioned anything about Devlin Raines. Was this a one-night stand? Was this a love affair? Even worse, did he rape her? I had no idea what the truth was anymore, and it rocked me to my core. How did I come to be?

Why didn't you tell me, Michael? In a rush, I pushed all of my feelings of anger and anguish out to him.

He didn't reply. He didn't need to.

Like a soft breeze, all of sudden I felt his presence near me. In a daze, I saw him hunch down next to me. I glanced at him quickly, hoping I could look away before the tears I was barely holding back came pouring forth. His expression was so apologetic, though, and so sad, I just couldn't stop them, and in an instant, they flooded my eyes and came streaming down my cheeks. Michael reached out to me and gently pulled me close. Cradling me against him, stroking my hair and pressing tender kisses to the top of my head as my emotions wrecked me inside.

Speaking softly in my ear, he told me he had guessed there might be a connection but was never sure of it. In his research, he had learned of a brief relationship Devlin had back in the early nineties with a local woman, but he didn't know the woman's name. After watching me for a time, he realized that I looked familiar to him. He found some photos of Devlin from years ago and thought there was a possibility we were related. However small that possibility was, he had been forced to investigate it.

"I had no idea he was your father, Celie. None. I would have spared you this. And if you *had* ever found out in the future, I wouldn't have wanted or planned on it being like this, I can promise you that." He held me close, resting his cheek against my hair.

I hiccupped. "Does he know?"

"I don't think so." Michael reached down and gingerly tilted my head up by my chin. Looking me in the eyes, he emphatically said, "I mean it, love. I wasn't trying to keep this from you. I didn't know."

I looked up at him after a minute, sure that my eyes were red and weary, but I was calmer knowing he was there. I gave him a half smile. "You called me 'love' again."

"Of course I did." He placed a gentle kiss on my lips.

I sniffled. "I looked for you earlier. You were gone."

"I wanted to go check out the warehouse. I thought it would be safer for you if I went alone."

"You weren't here," I whispered. "It hurt."

"I'm sorry."

"I—" I took a deep breath, feeling like I had been breathing shallow for too long. "I wanted to tell you something," I said, feeling worn down and tired. I laid my head against his chest and closed my eyes. "I wanted you to know, but you were gone."

"Know what, love?" He began stroking my hair again.

I was half awake but cozy and warm, snuggled up against his chest. I breathed in the scent of him, listening to his heartbeat and feeling his breath on my forehead. "That I love you," I mumbled into his chest.

Michael paused in his affections for a moment. I felt him take his own deep breath before pressing his lips to my temple and letting them linger there. After a moment, he said, "God help me, how much I love you, Celie."

He continued to stroke my hair and hold me close until I fell asleep in his arms.

After a long nap where I'm sure I drooled or snored, or did both, Michael told me about what he had found at the warehouse. The fence lining the warehouse lot was patrolled by at least six Sons and Daughters at a time, and cameras were in various locations for in-house surveillance. He knew that Devlin—my father, ick—was using the old manager's office as his own personal base of operations. The windows that would have let in light were boarded over with sheet metal, and Michael could see at least four guards posted inside and around the office. I wasn't sure how the hell we would get in there, but we had to try. Michael was hoping he could lure Devlin out of there, but we had no idea what we could use to do it. For now, our only plan was to get over there and hunker down in a nearby warehouse.

We gathered our things and loaded them back up into the car. Michael said goodbye to Xander before we left, telling him we were going camping together. I knew Michael hadn't told him about what we were doing, but that was okay—Michael had his reasons. Maybe when this was all said and done, he would let Xander in and find out he could trust a few more people with his secret.

I definitely liked Xander. He was a good guy, a nice guy, but there was something about him that set my Spidey senses tingling. It was clear he could be trusted to back us up if we needed him, but he was also holding something back. I was going to have to watch him.

On the road, I asked Michael if we could stop for something to eat. We grabbed some food from a local Taqueria, and as we left the parking lot, I broke into my chicken burrito. Oddly enough, as I leaned in to take a bite, I glanced in the side mirror and saw a gray car about four car lengths back that had really dark tinted windows. I stopped eating and eyed it for a minute, studying it to see if the driver followed our movements. After a left turn and a right, I knew we were being followed.

In between bites of burrito, I mumbled, "I hate to be the bearer of bad cliches, but we're being followed, Mike." I wrapped up my burrito. "It's a gray car, maybe three or four cars back."

"I see it. How did you know?"

"Well, something told me it wasn't normal. Besides, the windows are super dark, and I've seen plenty of movies with cars like that."

"Does that happen to you a lot? Getting vibes about things? Feelings about things?" He turned a corner and started going faster, the speedometer going from 45 to 50, 55 to 60...

"Sometimes. I get something sort of nudging my brain, like a tickle. Been happening for years."

"Hmm, interesting."

"Yeah, it helps me when I'm trying to judge a person's character."

"Didn't help you much with me," he said sarcastically.

I gave him a silly smile, sticking out my tongue and crossing my eyes. "Love makes everything fuzzy."

"Excuses, excuses."

I laughed at him as he sped even faster, the Chrysler now going about 80 miles per hour in a residential neighborhood.

"Oh, turn here!" I shouted and pointed to the right. He slowed just enough to make the turn and then hit the gas again. We dodged and weaved through Bantum, taking side streets and waiting to cross intersections until the lights turned yellow. It took some time, but we eventually lost them.

"You weren't kidding about your place being watched. Makes me wonder how many times they followed me."

"A lot," said Michael, and I looked at him. "I had to keep my distance when I watched you because they were everywhere those last two weeks."

"Really?"

"Yes. They were probably going to take you the day after I showed up."

"Well, I guess it's a good thing you showed up when you did. Otherwise, I'd probably be in that warehouse right now, roasting over an open flame with the natives poking at me with sharpened sticks." I picked up my burrito again, but—realizing I wasn't hungry anymore—I tossed it back in the bag.

"What I don't get is how he doesn't know who I am?" I turned in my seat to face Michael. "I mean, if you saw a resemblance, wouldn't he?"

"Not if he's so wrapped up in his mission to get to me. I'm his answer to everything—"

"—and I'm just a means to an end," I finished. I looked down at my hands and wondered if they were like Devlin's. I felt cold. "I don't want him to know," I whispered.

Michael whipped his head towards me. "He has to. He needs to know so he won't kill you. You're his legitimate daughter. Not one of these cult fanatics, but his own flesh and blood." He looked back at the road, but glanced at me again, waiting for my response.

"I don't mean shit to him!" I snapped, suddenly angry that I was being forced on someone I was supposed to hate—who I *did* hate.

"That's possible. But it's *also* possible that you do. Maybe when he finds out—"

"No! Listen to what I'm saying: I don't want him to know. Not where I am *or* who I am—none of it," I ground out. "If he can't remember knocking up my mother, then he doesn't deserve to know I exist." Looking out the window, I added, "It's just better that way."

Michael stayed silent for a few minutes before reaching over and placing his hand on top of my thigh. "I'm sorry for what you're going through right now, and I'm sorry to have to say this, but you can't hide from this. You can't hide from *him*. He's part of you, and I think he'll always be drawn to you." I glanced at him and he met my eyes for a moment. "I am not going to let him hurt you. And I firmly believe if he knows you're his child, it might stay his hand."

"I doubt it," I muttered under my breath.

"Please—trust me on this."

"No, Michael—not on this. Deep in my gut, I know telling him won't make any difference. I'm certain of it, and I believe you know it, too. Regardless of my blood, he'll still try to kill me if it means he can have yours."

I felt that same damn chill again. It was like the one I felt before Raines got into my head. However, this time I was prepared. This time, I would do everything to keep him from invading my body. I clenched my right fist between my seat and the door, ensuring Michael wouldn't see me digging my nails into my palm. I'd fight this asshole with every last breath I had.

"Besides," I murmured, returning to gaze out the window, "revenge is a dish best served cold."

Chapter Seven

No Matter the Cost

We drove down the highway into the outskirts of Bantum. New age music played on the radio, melancholy and mysterious, and I felt like I was in a movie on my way to the tragic climax. Michael headed to one of the empty warehouses nearby but not immediately next to the one that Devlin claimed. We parked his 300M inside and took out our gear. Climbing the steel staircase to the second floor, we made our camp in one of the smaller supervisor offices up top. I rolled out a giant olive-green sleeping bag as Michael pulled out two M.R.E.s for us. We ate and talked about small things, and he didn't try to mention revealing myself to Devlin again.

When we went to bed down for the night, I climbed into the sleeping bag first, with Michael settling in after me. I felt him wrap his arms around me, one draped over my side and stomach protectively, and the other under my head like a pillow. I closed my eyes and simply listened to him breathe, letting it soothe my soul.

"I won't let him hurt you," he said quietly against my ear.

"I know."

"You mean too much to me."

"Probably as much as you mean to me." I found his hand and entwined our fingers. "We have a plan, though. We'll kill him, the cult will fall apart, and all's well that ends well."

He chuckled. "You know—you don't sound as positive as you think you do."

"About what?"

"Any of it."

We lay in silence for a while, but it felt heavy. All the things I wasn't saying to him were weighing down on me. I had to tell him. I turned my head slightly. "Mike? Hey, are you still awake?"

"Of course. Are you ready to talk to me? I could hear the thoughts flitting about in your head—little wings of butterflies."

I laid my head back down on his arm and sighed. "I don't feel like I have a choice. I'm kind of suffocating myself by holding my breath all this time."

"I thought so. So what's worth dying for?"

"You." I felt his whole body stiffen in surprise. "Us, I mean. Listen, I know you don't want to talk about this—"

"You're right," he bit out.

"—but I think we need to. How can you expect us to be together if I'm going to get old? What if I get a disease?"

"We'll deal with that when the time comes."

I pushed myself away from him and turned over. I wanted him to see my face: I wanted to see his reaction when I asked, "And what happens when I die?"

His eyes darkened. "I don't know."

"What if it happened suddenly, like in a car accident—what then?"

"I... If you ever— I don't—"

"You *do* know, Michael." I leaned over and kissed him, gently, pouring all of my love into the kiss so he knew I was serious. I pulled back and whispered his name. "Michael. I love you. I want to be with you. I know that it's a sacrifice, but I'm willing to make it."

Michael stared at me, his eyes glowing silver against the black of the night.

"I'm ready."

His eyes flitted across my face. "I don't think I could do it. I love you too much to have you hate me."

"I won't hate you: I'm *asking* you for this. I know what it means, and I'm telling you that it's the right decision." He didn't move, just took a deep breath, and I felt his sorrow on the exhale.

In an instant, I realized what had been bothering him most about all of this, and I speared him with my eyes. "You're not Amelia. You're *not*. You aren't evil, and you aren't manipulative. You definitely aren't looking to score; although, I am okay with that last part if you are?"

Michael groaned. "I'm not kidding about this, Celie."

I angled my head, ensuring he could see my smile. "I know. I just want *you* to know that this is something I want, and I want it from you—*with* you. You won't be killing me. In fact, you'll be giving me a brand-new life with you, and it will make both of us very happy for a long, long time."

"There are parts of it that aren't what you think."

"Like what? No sunlight? Fake. No garlic? Definitely fake."

"Like the *hunger*."

"You've got that covered, haven't you?"

"There are things that can happen. Things you might do if my 'arrangement' falls through." He suddenly couldn't meet my eyes. "You won't like what the hunger makes you do."

I thought of that for a moment. "As long as you're with me, we can see through anything—*anything*. I'm sure of it, and you won't convince me otherwise." I leaned over him and placed a kiss on his lips. "Besides, you have to teach me the dream thing. I would love to get inside your head." I felt his arms encircle me, his body relaxing. We stayed like that for a time, me lying against him, his arms wrapped around me, and we merely took a few minutes to be together.

"I love you, Celie." His whisper in my ear was warm, and I shivered.

"Ah yes... Isn't love grand?"

A gravelly, menacing voice infiltrated our space, causing me to jump in surprise. I had heard that voice before, but this time, it wasn't in my head. It was in the room mere feet away from us, and it was just as evil as the last time.

Michael swiftly moved me so he could sit up and then pushed me behind him. I turned my head to see a man standing just inside the doorway. He was tall and thin, dressed all in black, and draped in a long trench coat. His hair was long and white, pulled back the way Michael would have done. Yet, despite the color of his hair, he didn't appear old at all. He looked youthful, but his features were angular and cold, with a strong Roman nose to accent his profile.

But his most striking feature was the color of his eyes. They were dark green—and just like mine.

Michael slowly rose to his feet, holding his hand out and helping me to my own. He kept me behind him, using his own body as a shield. "Hello, Raines."

"How are we today, Michael?" Devlin looked sinister, in the most twisted of ways, lips pursed in amusement. Standing casually, hands clasped at his back, he cocked his head to the side and acted like he was peering around Michael. "Ah, I see you have your *friend* with you. Do stand up, child." When I refused to move, smirked. "Come, Michael—bring her forward so I can have a look." He smiled, and it looked entirely too practiced.

Pleasantries were not his strong suit.

I clenched onto Michael's shirt, scared but feeling the anger rising in me. I wanted to pummel this man, tear him from limb to limb. His presumption, his arrogance, and his patronizing attitude were enough to convince me this pseudo-human being was the devil incarnate. Vampire or not, he needed to die.

Sensing my anger, Michael reached around and pressed me closer to him. "Why are you here?"

Devlin feigned shock. "Why am *I* here? Why are *you* here?"

When Michael said nothing, Devlin tittered. "You really thought you could sneak up on me, eh?"

"Tell us what you want," demanded Michael. "Stop with your childish games and be out with it."

Devlin's smile faltered. "Rodger and Gerald advised me—as you undoubtedly requested—that you would be coming to see me." His face became emotionless. "I thought I would come to you instead."

Feeling snarky, I called out, "Great. Thanks. You can leave now."

Devlin ignored me. "We have so much to discuss, Michael—you and I. Why don't we sit down and talk?"

Michael was getting angrier by the second. "You know there isn't anything I want to discuss with you."

"I doubt that. I'm sure you have a number of things to say to me." Devlin's smile returned, and all I could see was a row of pristine white teeth. "By the way, how *is* Ginny doing these days?"

I wasn't the only one shocked and appalled at his blatant rage bait. Michael's chest rumbled beneath my hands, and I knew he was moments away from ripping Devlin's throat out.

"Has she learned to walk again? I *so* enjoyed the time we spent together. She really was quite charming." He lowered his head and grinned, looking up at us from beneath hooded eyes. "You know, I've been a little bored lately. Perhaps I owe her a visit?"

Michael snarled, outraged and nearly rushing at him. His anger was barely contained, at the brink of boiling over.

I held him back. "Don't do it, Michael. He's baiting you—he *wants* you to do it," I whispered.

"Yes, listen to her, Michael." Devlin's face was smug as he mocked me, and I started fantasizing about shredding it to pieces. "Obviously she's a smart girl," he mused before turning his attention back to me. "Please step forward. Maybe you and I could chat and find out what it is that's bothering him so?" He gestured in invitation.

Teeth gritted, I ground out, "Go fuck yourself."

Devlin tried to frown, but it only managed to make him look worse. "Hmm. Not very good manners, child." He shook his index finger at me. "Tsk tsk."

"Like I could give a rat's ass what you think," I replied sharply.

"Indeed." The smile slipped from Devlin's face, and a dark shadow overcame his features. "I could teach you to respect me."

"Just try it, asshole."

I felt Michael's grip tighten as his thoughts entered my head. *If he comes towards us, I'm taking you out of here.*

No! If he comes, we fight him. I'm not leaving you to do it alone—ever. You haven't fought him since he changed. You don't know what he's like now.

I can handle it.

"What will it be, Michael? Will you come with me so we can get down to business? Or do I need to take her from you?" Everything about Devlin was threatening violence now. I felt the air in the room change, and the temperature dropped rapidly; it scared the hell out of me. He was drawing energy into himself, and I knew something was going to happen—and it was going to be bad. I pulled at Michael's shirt, tensing.

"I'll kill you before that happens," Michael growled.

"Prove it."

Then Devlin disappeared.

"Oh Christ," I moaned. Just as I felt something tug on the back of my shirt, Michael spun around and yanked me forward. Before I could blink, we vanished.

A millisecond later, I fell into the passenger seat of the Chrysler, and Michael was already hitting the gas.

"What the hell is happening? How could he do that porting thing that you do? You tell me how he got that through his 'bioengineering' thingie!"

Devlin appeared in front of the car.

The brakes squealed as Michael pressed them into the floorboard. Throwing it into reverse, he clenched his jaw and sped backwards. Shifting back into drive, the car kicked up dirt and gravel as it flew.

"I don't know. Fuck! This is bad. This is so fucking bad."

I pushed up my sleeves, checking myself for any injuries. Nothing. Still reeling from what happened in the office, I turned around in the leather seat and gripped the side of it to hold myself at the new angle. I watched the warehouses get smaller as we drove beyond them, keeping an eye out to see if anyone was following.

"Mike, I'm really confused about all of this. You said he was a vampire, that he took your DNA and made himself into one."

"Right."

"Are you *absolutely* sure?"

"Pretty damn sure. He found some of my blood on the pavement in that parking lot and he used it to turn himself into one."

I took my eyes away from the warehouses in the growing distance and focused on him. "But are you a hundred percent positive?"

"What are you getting at?"

"Is there any possibility—any at all—that he found some *other* way to become more than a man?"

Michael spared me a quick glance, then focused on taking corners and pushing the car's limits to drive even faster. "I don't know," he said. "None that I know of."

"But we both know that demons can move like that, right?"

"Yeah." Michael glanced at me. I was tapping my fingertip on my lips, deep in thought. "Wait—are you suggesting what I think you're suggesting?"

"Probably," I muttered. I let my thoughts settle into place and placed my hands on the center console. As clearly as I could, I explained myself.

"Ok. Check this out. So what I'm thinking now—and just hear me out on this—is if maybe he's *not* a vampire?" While I was talking, my eyes kept darting to the perimeter of the car for flying trench coats or whirlwinds with white hair. Seriously, I had no idea what to expect at this point. "What if—and this even sounds bizarre to me—but what if he's actually gotten some lower-level demon shit kind of infusion? Is that— Could he do that? Is that even possible?"

"I've never heard of it. I thought conducting DNA experimentation was the worst of it, but considering his work..." Michael's voice trailed off. "If he got a hold of a demon, somehow managed to cage it and to inject himself with its blood or some cellular material... Yeah, maybe he could have warped himself into something not unlike a half-breed."

I looked at him closely. "So now we're talking about a half-*demon*?"

"It's...it's a probable theory."

"My father—Asshole Extraordinaire—might be part demon, and I—"

"Might be," Michael interjected. "The key word there is 'might.' We don't know if that's really what's going on with him."

"Jesus," I muttered, "I am so not ready for this." Facing forward now, I watched the road with him.

Arriving back at the office, he parked in the back. It was early morning now. We had taken numerous backroads to avoid being followed again, circling out of the northern end of the city and coming back in from the south. Michael put the car in park and I climbed over to straddle him. Sitting back across his thighs, I said, "So how do we do this?"

"I thought you would know that by now, Celie," he said, seductively arching an eyebrow.

"That's not what I mean." I let him see my thoughts.

"Are you serious? You wanna do this *now*? Really?"

"Really really. I mean, why not? After what we just encountered, it seems as good a time as any, right?"

"I don't know. Maybe," he mumbled to himself. He ran his left hand back through his hair. It was hanging down loosely, and I was dying to run my own fingers through it. "Maybe," he repeated. "We are going to go fight everyone soon, so this could be the appropriate time..."

"Well, how long does this take? Will I be out of commission or something?"

"No, not really. I just didn't know you were planning on doing it here—in the fucking car."

"Car, office, bed: makes no difference to me!"

He grumbled, and I used my nicest, sweetest tone. "C'mon, handsome. This'll be easy." He looked at me like I had three heads, so I crossed my arms in front of me and huffed. "Michael, we're doing this. If I can have even the smallest margin of your abilities going into this, that would be helpful, don't you think?"

"You will *definitely* be the end of me," he groaned.

"You know it," I said confidently.

Michael dragged his hands over his face and sighed. "Okay, you win. We'll do it now. But I want it on record that you chose the car." He took a deep breath and then looked at me with those shining eyes of his. "Come here."

I leaned forward a little bit, and he suddenly grabbed me by the back of my neck. Pulling me toward him, he kissed me—hard. There was a primal passion in it—a craving. I found his shoulders and dug my fingers into him, hanging on. I felt him nip my lower lip and shuddered. He broke our kiss and looked right in my eyes. I felt flushed from head to toe.

"Are you sure about this?" he asked quietly.

"Absolutely," I said, bracing myself for him to dive in. In a second, something came over me and it was intense—exquisite even. A raging pleasure like I couldn't believe—and had no idea was possible—swept through my body. I closed my eyes and felt it wash over me, again and again, and in my mind's eye, I saw Michael beckoning me. We met in a rush of naked flesh there, and it felt dangerous and intoxicating.

Share yourself with me... Give yourself to me...

I opened my eyes to see him staring at me hungrily. Without awareness of what I was doing—without thinking at all—I bared my neck and shoulder for him, letting the open collar of my shirt rest lazily just above my breasts. I licked my lip before biting it, and I watched his eyes smolder as he watched me do it. Slowly, he leaned forward and kissed me, deliberately sensual, and intensely intimate. With his hands holding onto my hips, his lips gradually moved downward, trailing a path along my jaw and down my neck with his lips. I felt his tongue trace across my collarbone, and I could feel his breath, warm against my skin. I reached around him and into his hair. I let myself wander, enjoying the silky feel of it running through my fingers, and then I clutched a handful and pulled. At my instigation, his grip tightened, a growl rumbled low in his throat, and he bit down.

At first, there was the sensation of pain, sharp as his teeth pierced me; but then, there was the sensation of pleasure, overwhelming and decadent. I felt loved and desired as I was killed. As Michael drank from me, I weakened: my body was dying. I tried to hold onto him—tried to keep my hand in his hair and my fingers on his skin—but

I just didn't have the strength. I didn't need to worry, though, because he held me close and lovingly, like he was afraid I might break—and only he could make me shatter. It went on and on, like falling in a dream. My vision darkened, like the end of a movie, starting from the outside and working its way into the center of the frame. My breathing faltered, and a new kind of cold began to seep into my frame.

Before my eyesight left me completely, I saw Michael pull back and look at me, concern and worry mixed with love in his eyes. I couldn't speak. I tried to smile, to let him know that it was okay. I wanted him to know I was happy he did this for me, but I just didn't have the energy. I think he knew, though, because he bent down and kissed me sweetly. My own blood stained my lips, and I stopped resisting. I went to sleep in his arms again.

I was dead.

The world welcomed me back in a couple of hours. I jolted awake and was instantly blinded by the sunlight. I wanted to scream but couldn't find my voice just yet. A hoarse and violent whisper erupted from my throat.

"Shit! Sorry. I'm sorry about that."

I hurriedly sat up, and Michael was there, draping a blanket over me. He wrapped it around me carefully, the wool itching me mercilessly as it touched any exposed skin. Michael smoothed the hair back from my face. "Are you alright?"

I was feeling panicky, edgy, like something was going to jump out at me any moment, and my skin felt like it was crawling with unseen insects. I couldn't focus clearly on him, which bugged the crap out of me, and my nose was filled with the scent of metal—like copper from a penny. Was a lightning storm brewing? On top of it all, I could also hear a soft hum coming from him, and that was more than a little disturbing. I reached out to him, and he grabbed my hands.

"It's okay, Celie. I'm here. Everything that you're feeling is completely normal."

I tried to whisper to him, my breath barely making it out of me. "My...voice..." I squeaked.

"That will come back soon. Your body is still adjusting to everything." He tucked another loose strand behind my ear. "It takes effort to come back from the dead."

"Can't see you..." I managed and then choked, painfully, like my throat was raw. I felt helpless, weak, and beyond vulnerable. I was half the person I had been before. I wanted to rip my skin off to make the itching bug-like sensation go away. If I could have, I would have loved nothing more than to scream—if anything, just to hear my own voice. And the humming! The goddamn humming! It just wouldn't *stop!* If it kept going, I was going to stab myself in the ear; I just knew it.

"I know. I promise, it's only temporary."

I followed the sound of him, reaching out, and letting out a little moan when he took my hands in his.

"Some of what you're feeling is from the change," he assured me. "Other parts of it—and I know this is going to be hard on you so soon—some of this can only go away by drinking."

I froze. I wasn't ready to bite someone else. Hell, did I even have the teeth to do it, yet? I pushed myself back from him, trying to scoot away.

Michael took hold of me by my upper arms and held me still. "You need to do this, Celie. It's the only thing that's going to help you."

"Can't... bite." I tried to look at his face, but I still couldn't see him; he was simply a blurry shape.

"You don't have to," he replied calmly. Michael was prepared. "I brought some extra just in case. Here." He reached past me and pulled out something large and cylindrical and brought it to my lips. I brought my hands up, and he helped me balance it as I tipped it gingerly towards my mouth.

I darted my tongue out to get the smallest taste, unsure if I would be able to stand it. That hadn't occurred to me before, whether I would be comfortable with the taste, but I would do anything for this man. To my surprise, blood was sweet and heavy like concentrated fruit juice, and I took small swallows from the container. Within a few minutes, most of the agonizing sensations had dissipated. My skin had stopped crawling, and that low whirring I had heard coming from Michael faded away.

"Better?"

"Yes," I said, and startled myself by speaking normally. I grabbed my throat. "I can talk!" I shouted out.

"Yeah. Your eyes will be better soon, too."

"Thank god for that. I was going crazy not being able to speak." I wanted to feel him, though, desperately. I opened my arms, and he came right into them. I held him close, knowing that no matter what, we could always be together. I sighed against him and closed my eyes.

Beneath my cheek, I felt his chest rumble as he spoke. "You don't hate me? Hate what I've done to you?"

I tried to pull back but he held me close, as if he couldn't bear to have me look at him. "Of course not. Thank you for giving me this." I turned my head and pressed a kiss to his shoulder. "I know it was hard for you, but I mean it. This was a *gift* you've given me, not a curse. You and I can always be together, and I thank you for that."

Michael released the tension in his body, his frame relaxing beneath my hands, and rested his chin on my head. His hair was still loose, and it fell around me like a warm, protective embrace.

A few minutes later, I was checking myself for changes. Nothing looked different to me. My tattoos were still on my skin, my scars were still where they had been. I reached around and pulled some of my hair forward. It was still my hair. For all intents and purposes, I looked...normal? Except for the whole vampire thing, of course.

Michael helped me out of the car, and we headed into the shop. It was still safe, and there were no signs of cult invasion. In fact, Xander was still there and preparing to close up for lunch. I bum-rushed him at the door while Michael was distracted, dragging him by a handful of his shirt and forcing him to follow me upstairs to the third floor. Michael followed in hot pursuit, unsure of what was going on.

Xander was staring at me, perplexed by my urgency. Then his brow knit together, and he looked me up and down in a strange examination. I could tell he was curious as to why I was a bit different than the day before. I was like one of those picture puzzles, where six things look the same but one of them is subtly different.

Pick out which part of Celie is not like the others!

Right as he opened his mouth, I said, "It's a long story, and I actually think it's one you're entitled to." Turning to Michael, I thought, *You need to tell him.*

Michael's eyes widened. *What?! No. I'm not dragging him into this.*

So it would be better for him to be killed by a demon hybrid without ever knowing who his friend really was? Are you kidding me?

Michael's brow furrowed. *I'm not jeopardizing my friendship with him. We can protect him. He doesn't have to know; I can just send him away.*

Shut up.

What do you—

Shut. Up. I stared him down, ignoring that Xander was further confused by the obviously strange looks we were giving each other. *You can't live like this, not trusting anyone. I know you had your reasons, but this is different.*

Michael glared at me. *How is this different?*

"He could be killed if you don't tell him what's going on. Now stop being so stubborn and tell him." I jerked my thumb at Xander. "He needs to know. He *deserves* to know."

Xander gaped at us. "What the hell is going on, man? Someone wants to kill me?" When no one answered, he grew angry. "What is this? What do I need to know?"

"Christ, Celie!" Michael was exasperated and frustrated at being put on the spot.

"Tell him," I demanded. Through my thoughts, I added, *If you really are his friend, you'll tell him, no matter the cost to yourself.*

Michael was a touch angry, staring me down like I had thrown him under the bus. I know he was stunned that I was accusing him of being selfish, but it was the truth. He was scared, afraid to lose a friend he had garnered through years of secrecy; however, in light of the present situation, he had to come clean. I jerked my eyes toward Xander, and Michael looked over at him. Xander was still standing there, his arms folded across his chest, and he looked completely lost.

Michael deflated a little as he pushed his ego aside. He walked over to Xander and put his hand on his shoulder. "She's right. We need to talk." Steering him around, the two of them walked to the back of the floor where they sat down across from each other. I went back downstairs to give them some privacy.

I was waiting for probably thirty minutes or so when Xander came downstairs. I was sitting on top of a table, sipping my 'fruit juice' from a mug, reading through one of Chaucer's works, and I looked up when he reached the bottom step. The first thing I noticed was that Michael wasn't with him. He walked over, stopping in front of me, standing tall, confident, and pissed off. He gestured to me wildly. "I suppose you're going to tell me you're one of them, too, huh? That the way of it?"

I put the mug down next to the open book on my left. Resting my palm on top of the book, I looked right at him. "Yeah. Today I am."

Xander huffed. "Oh. Oh, 'today you are'..." He shook his head, hands on his hips for a minute. All of a sudden, he stepped forward and got right in my face. "I don't know who you are, little girl—"

"Little girl?"

"—but you have royally fucked with my friend's head! I've known that man for twelve years—twelve *long* fucking years—and he's *never* mentioned any of the crazy bullshit he just threw at me up there. What kind of game are you running? Are you after his money? Is that it? Going after the rich guy? Think you can land yourself a free ticket?" He was fuming.

With serious effort, I stood my ground. I was burning up, seeing red, ready to explode. I was one hundred percent pissed off that he would betray Michael's trust like this.

Keeping my voice steady, I replied, "You better watch what you say—about me and Michael. On that note, you better watch what you accuse me of, too. Someone might think that you wanted me to kick your ass."

"I'd love to see you try, woman! I oughta kick *your* ass for doing this to him! He's totally convinced that he can—that he's a, a— Shit! He's up there thinking he's some kind of motherfucking Dracula or some shit!"

I stared him down, lowering the volume of my voice until he could barely hear it. "Has he ever lied to you?"

Xander froze, the thought having never crossed his mind. Yet an instant later, his own voice dropped down low, but it was seething with anger. "Don't even think you can make me feel guilty about this. He's messed up—*you* messed him up. You should be the one to feel like shit."

I leapt forward, putting my face in his with no fear and no nervousness whatsoever. Still keeping my voice calm and monotone, I said, "If you want to blame someone, fine—blame me. But you'll be the one who's an asshole for turning your back on him." He went to argue, but I didn't give him the chance. "Don't you get it? He didn't *want* to tell you. He knew you wouldn't believe him, and he was afraid to lose you as a friend. I thought it was better for you to know what was coming after you. How dumb was I to think you would be a decent friend and stand with him to fight? But look at you," I sneered, showing him how disgusted I was at his reaction. "You stand there and call yourself a friend—*his friend*—but at the first sign of a problem, you run. You, sir, are a fucking coward."

Xander pulled back his fist, ready to punch a hole right through my head. I just stood there, waiting for it, knowing with my new abilities he could do just about anything, and I would live. I could have left it at that, but that just wasn't my style: I pressed on.

"I know what this is, you know. It's not that you think he's lying. It's not that you think I put some story in his head. Oh no. What's really going on is that you don't want to believe him because it would mean you'd have to open your eyes. Your precious little world would come crumbling down around you, leaving you open and exposed. You think you're safe? You think the only thing that can hurt big, bad you is disease? An accident? Think again, jackass."

I reached out and grabbed his shirt, yanking him right up into my face. His fists unclenched automatically as his hands came up and tried to pull himself out of my grip. It was no use, though: I was much stronger now. I inhaled the scent of his very real fear, the kind that lay deep down and left him scared of the unknown.

I could also hear the blood rushing in his veins.

"Devils and demons do exist. Michael and I are fighting them." I smiled, feeling my teeth elongate as I gave in to the heady call of his blood. As I showed him my new set of teeth, his eyes widened, and the whites became fully visible around his pupils. "You better get your head out of your ass and be the goddamn person Michael thinks you are."

I shoved Xander away from me, and he landed in a pile of boxes. "Sorry," I muttered. "I don't have a handle on my strength yet."

I went to walk past him, and he stopped me, taking hold of my left arm. I looked down at his hand, then up at his face. He was still angry, but something else was there, something that told me my words clicked for him somehow. I paused.

"You're not kidding...are you?" His voice was smaller now, his puzzled frustration fading, and potential belief was creeping in. I chose to continue staring at him and saying nothing. What was I going to say that hadn't already been said?

Xander turned away from me and went over to sit down on the tabletop, his pride crumpling in defeat. He slouched over, his elbows on his knees while he cradled his head in his hands. I watched him for a minute, breathing and fighting to understand as he struggled to accept it all. I walked over and hopped back up to sit on the table next to him.

"You gonna hold it together or pass out?" I asked him, curious to see if he had any attitude change.

"I got this," he mumbled. "I got this." A second later, he added, "I just don't like it."

"What's to like? Besides, you're not the one with the half-demon for a father."

Xander jerked up. "A *what*?"

"Yeah, found that out today. My father is probably a half-demon." I shrugged. "Go figure."

Xander just sat there, gaping at me. I laughed a little. "It's okay. We're gonna kill him, so you don't have to worry." I patted his knee. "We'll protect you."

"Screw you. I can take care of myself."

"Not if you don't believe." I gave him the most serious face I could muster. "Listen, Xander. There are things in this world that I would've written off as bullshit a few days ago. Now my world is upside-down, inside-out. It feels safer to believe that things like this aren't real, that they're just crazy thoughts in someone's head. It always feels blissful to live in that kind of ignorance, where you have no worries and no dangers. You walk around, day-to-day, thinking you're invincible; nothing can touch you. Nuclear war in your town? Impossible. Monsters under your bed? Ridiculous. But once you find out...when you've seen these evil things in the flesh...it's a hell of a lot safer to believe so you can prepare to fight it."

He scoffed. "I know all of this. I just... Goddamn—how do I accept vampires? Or demons?"

"Well, get crackin' 'cause we don't have a lot of time. Michael needs you to believe in him—now—yesterday, even. Devlin's not gonna stop until he's destroyed everything Michael has in his life, and that includes you, sir."

Xander regarded me, taking it all in, and I waited. I sat patiently, even though it tested me. After a moment or two, he tilted his head back and let out a huge sigh, looking towards the ceiling but not really seeing it. He ran his hand over his smooth head, his thoughts tumbling around inside of it: I could tell he was trying to get them to come together, but we just didn't have that kind of time.

"So?"

He looked at me out of the corner of his eye, his head still angled back. He looked away and said, "I'm his friend. I'm not giving that up."

"Damn good thing, dude. I was getting ready to smack you around, break your jaw or somethin'."

He laughed instinctively, bending his head back down to look at me. "Damn woman!"

"What can I say? I don't have a lot of patience for this."

He paused for a moment and said, "Do you love him?"

"Well, that's a stupid question."

"Just answer me. I need to hear you say it."

"I do. I love him. I love Michael."

"Thank you."

"Don't thank me yet. Do I need to go upstairs and clean up the mess you made?"

"No," he said, and I could see him silently berating himself. "No, I can do that myself."

I watched him march up the stairs, disappearing at the top. I sent out my thoughts and told Michael to expect a visitor.

While they were upstairs, I resumed maintaining a vigil on the first floor. I was in the back of the shop, eyeing the antiques when I heard a jingle, like a bell or something similar clanging up front. I wasn't sure if Michael had anything attached to the front door, something to alert his staff of shoppers. I began making my way back up front, weaving around tables set out with books and sculptures.

Halfway there, something slammed into my right shoulder from the front, heavy and invisible. The hit spun me around, and I fell hard, landing face-down against the wood floor. I could feel something on top of me, holding me down, but I couldn't see it. Then I felt pressure sliding up my back, and within seconds, there was a warm, wet tongue slinking across the edge of my right ear. I choked back the bile that instantly rose up in my throat. Hot breath feathered my ear, rank and putrid. I struggled, desperate to escape the vomit-inducing sensations. I couldn't breathe, the weight pressing down on me everywhere, and even though I tried not to panic, I could feel it creeping in. It was strong—so very strong—and despite my own new strength, I couldn't dislodge it.

Then this *thing*—the invisible force with a wet tongue—spoke to me, and I screamed in my mind to Michael. My thoughts were nothing but a mindless, never-ending scream.

Devlin was here.

Chapter Eight

It's Probably a Trap

Remaining intimately close, he whispered, "Hush, child. I came to tell you that I have something that belongs to you. Something important." He nipped my ear, and I flinched, my stomach turning. "If you want it back, you need to listen to me."

I stayed silent, trying to cooperate or at least buy some time for Michael to get downstairs with Xander.

"Good girl," said Devlin softly. "I want you to bring Michael to me, to my warehouse."

"No."

I felt his hand jerk my chin, and pain blazed across the back of my neck. "He and I need to have a discussion, and he just never seems to have the time."

"Busy schedule," I said dryly. "I'm sure he could pencil you in for the next century."

No question in his tone, Devlin said, "He's told you what I want from him, I take it?"

"Yeah. You want to make other vampires, but you can't get it up."

This time, his hand wrapped around my neck and squeezed. The air I was already fighting for was nearly cut off entirely. "Oh, I can 'get it up', little one." He licked my ear again, and I nearly retched. "Would you like me to prove it to you?"

"You want his blood," I wheezed, changing the subject to get him back on track.

He relaxed his grip a little. "I knew he told you. Yes, dear, I want his blood. More than that, I want his gift. I need it."

"You want to curse people."

"I love my people," said Devlin matter-of-factly. "I want to give all of them his gift."

"You'll never have it. He'll never give it to you."

"Yes," he sighed. "I'm beginning to get the feeling that he doesn't like me. I wonder why?"

"Probably because you're an asshole," I managed, then clamped my mouth shut. I was wondering why Michael wasn't down here already. *Michael!*

Devlin chuckled. "He can't hear you." I had forgotten he could get inside my head. Damnit. "I told you before, girl," he said, his tone low, stern, and menacing, "I can teach you proper respect."

"You can take my respect and shove it up your—"

"Ah ah ah," Devlin admonished. "Any more of that from you, and you'll never see her again."

I froze. "See who?"

"Oh yes, the important—yet missing—piece of the puzzle." I could sense him smiling down at me as he eased even closer, his lips grazing my cheek. His fangs were visible from the outermost corner of my eye. "I have your friend back at my home. She's quite lovely, and I must say that I have enjoyed her company immensely."

I felt my stomach drop, but I feigned ignorance. "Friend?"

"I believe you call her, Kat?"

I screamed out loud this time, struggling with all of my newfound strength to get Devlin off me: I wanted to tear him apart.

Kat... Oh my god, Kat...

I had to get to her. She needed to get out of there; I needed to get her out of there. Screaming again, I heard footsteps running. Michael ported in across the floor, his fast, darting movement easily visible to me now, and I heard him roar as loud as a freight train.

"Remember what I said, dear. Bring him to my warehouse, and you'll get back your precious Kat." I felt him press a kiss to my neck, and then the weight disappeared.

I shoved against the floor and flipped over. I cried out, and Michael rushed over, skidding to a halt beside me. He knelt down and pulled me in close, wrapping his arms around me. Clinging to him, I felt fear and anger waging a war inside of me. He checked me everywhere for injuries while I watched Xander reach the bottom of the stairs, his hand still on the rail. He looked anxious, worried. I pulled back from Michael, and he helped me stand up.

"Are you hurt? Did he hurt you? Why didn't you call for me?"

"I did," I mumbled. "It didn't work."

Not giving a thought to myself or my state, I said, "Devlin has Kat." I struggled to keep my tears in check. So much had happened and learning that my best friend had been taken by this lunatic butcher was pushing me to the brink. Was this my fault? Was it because I called her? I couldn't know. I just knew she needed to be rescued as soon as possible. I couldn't let her wind up like Ginny.

"Kat? Who's Kat?" asked Xander.

"Wait—you mean your friend, Kat?" clarified Michael. "The one you live with?"

"Yes."

"Why?"

"He's holding her hostage. He said I have to bring you to him," I said, looking into Michael's eyes. We stared at each other, my love for him warring with my love for my surrogate sister. He knew what happened to Ginny, and the idea of that happening to another person, let alone someone I considered to be like a sister, enraged him.

"Well, you can't do it," said Xander. Both of us turned to him. "You can't give in to him. You know what he's going to do with what you're carrying."

"So what—now it's a virus?" I snarked, my anger feeding my sarcasm.

"It's how I'm dealing with it, okay?" he retorted angrily before turning to Michael. "You can't let him get a hold of it, Mike. None of us will be able to live in that kind of world."

"We know that," he ground out, his anger palpable. "But we can't let Kat suffer there with Devlin. He'll destroy her. There will be nothing left of her when he's done."

"I didn't say we would. From the sound of things, this guy is the King of Evil, but he'll be even more powerful if he has you. We can't let you fall into his hands."

"What are you suggesting then?" I asked him, a smidge calmer knowing that he wasn't suggesting we leave Kat with Devlin.

"A rescue mission. Just you and me." He pointed at me—and I was inclined to agree—but Michael stepped in between us.

"No. You are *not* taking her out there without me. The two of you can't face him alone."

"She's stronger now that she's like you, right? We'll have each other's backs out there, me and her. Once we get her girl, we'll move like lightning and get the hell outta there." Xander looked at me and I nodded, agreeing with his plan. I was itching to leave; we had to get her away from him. There was no telling what she had already gone through.

"I don't like this," said Michael.

I placed a hand on his arm and urged him to look at me. "What's to like? Each second we stand here and debate it, she's out there—"

I pointed out the window. "—alone, and with *him*." Michael stared down at me, his eyes worried. I knew he was envisioning Ginny. I took his face in my hands. "You and I both know we won't be able to live with ourselves if anything happens to her, if he does it again. Please—let me go save her."

Love lit up his eyes even as his face darkened. "Go." He shook a finger at me. "If anything happens, you call for me."

"What if Devlin blocks it again?" I asked worriedly. It panicked me to know that our intimate link could easily be dropped in on or denied. It was comforting to have, kind of like a personal lifeline.

"I don't know how he did it, but I'm going to see that it doesn't happen again." Michael reached out and took my face in both of his hands. "Call for me."

"I promise," I said and lifted up on my toes to kiss him. He put everything he was feeling into it, all his frustration, his love, and his worry. I gently pulled away and turned to Xander. "Let's go."

We grabbed a few things from the trunk of the 300M, including some silver bullets and handguns. Then I climbed into Xander's Charger and headed off to the industrial park. It tore my heart out to watch Michael disappear in the reflection of the car mirror.

Riding in silence, I watched the dashed lines on the road tick by, making myself sick and dizzy. It wasn't just that, though; I already felt that way from the situation. Uncomfortable and even twitchy, I was nervous about going into this without Michael. I knew he would be listening, and I knew he could port in at any time. However, knowing that Devlin could possibly prevent my call made me second guess all of Michael's abilities, especially the ones that would help him rescue me if I needed it. I hoped he didn't have to. I wanted to be able to go in, grab Kat, and bail out without Devlin even getting an inkling it was happening.

More importantly, I didn't want Devlin to realize I was a vampire. I didn't think he knew that I had been re-born; at least, I hoped he didn't. The possibility he could use my blood instead of Michael's made me nervous. I hadn't voiced my concerns, didn't think it had occurred to either of them, and I thought it was best it hadn't. *That could put us all one step ahead of him.* If I could keep my thoughts in check, possibly erect some mental fortress to keep him out, then maybe we could surprise him, take him on together. However, it all depended on keeping my initiation into that world a secret.

I looked over at Xander, who was intently focused on the road. I didn't know him very well, wasn't sure if he could be counted on, or even if he was really a Son in disguise. *Is he a double agent?* He had known Michael for twelve years, and he wasn't wrong—twelve years was a long time—but there was no way of knowing if he had remained loyal all that time. I wanted to believe he was reliable and trustworthy, and I know he wouldn't have gotten so crazy about our situation if he didn't care about Michael. I just wasn't sure, and I didn't want to make any mistakes with this. If he wasn't who I thought he was, if he wasn't who Michael thought he was, Kat could die, and the world could go to shit.

After all, it really was a matter of life and death.

Carefully choosing my words, I said, "So what kind of experience do you have with guns?"

"What's that?"

"I asked if you had any experience with guns. You know—military, firing ranges, and so on?"

"I was in the Army back in the day. Just the four years, but that's about it."

"You think you'll be able to handle the ones we brought?"

"I guess we'll find out."

"Yeah, I guess so..." I muttered. Louder, I asked, "You sure you're up for this?"

"Up for what?"

"You know, fighting demons and killing brainwashed, innocent people if necessary?"

"That what we're doing?"

"Yeah."

"Didn't know this would be happenin' when I woke up this morning."

I smirked. "None of us did, Xander."

"Do I actually have a choice, though?"

"Yes," I replied, then frowned. "And no. You could leave me behind, escape, disappear into the world and never look back. But it would find you some day. *He* would find you someday..."

"Guess I'm gonna get dirty, then."

"It's gonna be rough. I'm not sure what the extent of Devlin's powers actually is. Guns may not take care of it."

"I thought they had the same powers?" Xander asked.

"I don't think they are, to be honest." His answers were bizarre, not confirming or denying anything. Plus, he almost seemed to insinuate that he knew what Michael's powers were. I didn't think he'd been given all that information yet; even I wasn't sure of the full extent of what Michael could do, for that matter. I watched Xander cautiously, testing him for any sign that he was a cult spy. "I'm glad you're helping us."

"You can't pass on friendship because someone changes."

"Well, actually, he's always been a vampire. The only thing that changed was your perception of him."

"I suppose so."

"Do you still trust him?" I probed.

He grunted. "Maybe. We'll... We'll see what happens."

"I mean, I know you probably think he lied to you, but he was just trying to protect you—and himself. He was worried about your reaction."

"I'm okay."

"Good," I said. "Glad to hear it."

Through that whole conversation, Xander didn't meet my eyes once.

I went back to watching the road. I hated that entire conversation. All of his answers were cryptic, short, shallow, and without substance. It bothered me, giving me a nagging feeling in my gut that he was keeping something from me. Keeping my misgivings to myself, I stored our awkward exchange in the back of my mind. I didn't want him to know that I was having such suspicions about him. The rest of this trip, I was going to keep a close eye on him.

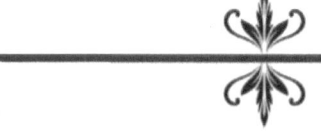

We got to the industrial park just after dark, the afterglow of the sun leaving the western sky a dark lavender. Xander drove quietly, lights off, and around to the building to the southeast of the warehouse. We knew which one it was because Michael had told us before we left. Parking between two large electric transformers that sat behind the building, we used them as a sort of camouflage. Opening our doors, we both went to the trunk, gearing up with our weapons. I grabbed the night-vision goggles I snatched from the 300M. They came equipped with an optical zoom feature I thought might help us better surveil the warehouse. After stashing two of the guns on me, I grabbed a switchblade and stuffed it down into the ankle of my left black boot.

I knew I had worn them for a reason.

Fixing Xander with a serious look, I asked, "Are you ready?"

He nodded. "Game on."

"Follow me," I said, and we headed out, sneaking over to the warehouse. We used cover wherever and whenever we could, not knowing if we could be seen in the dark by the bad guys or not. Hunched low, we scurried like rats traveling across a field of landmines, turning this way and that. Sometimes we had to move backward to go forward. To be honest, I wasn't positive that Devlin didn't have real landmines positioned strategically throughout the area.

Behind a pile of steel beams and mesh wiring, I paused, taking out the night-vision goggles. We were close, less than 100 feet from the perimeter of the building. I was crouched down in the dirt, holding the goggles to my eyes, and trying to locate the security cameras. I found them easily, but the guards were trickier. Scanning the fence left to right, all I could see were two of them standing by a corner, rifles slung over their shoulders. They were chatting away like they *didn't* work for a demonic, egomaniacal scientist. I kept looking for more but couldn't find any more of them. I brought down the goggles, then handed them over to Xander.

Pointing ahead, I said, "See the two over there?"

He raised them to his eyes. "Yeah, I see 'em."

"Do you see anymore?"

"Uh...no."

"Damn, there has to be more of them out there."

"Doesn't look like it."

"I don't like this. It feels...off?" I glanced at him. "I'm thinking it's a trap."

Silence ticked away. "So what do you want to do?" Xander asked, bringing down the goggles to look at me.

I shrugged. "Guess we'll just have to do this. I mean, what else can we do, right?" I watched him from the corner of my eye, keeping my gaze pointed at the building but feeling somehow like my greatest danger was right next to me.

"Nothing really. We have to go in. We need to get your friend back."

"God. I hope she's okay," I said to myself. I felt my palms beginning to sweat and wiped them on my black jeans.

"I'm sure she is," he said, and he sounded so confident, so self-assured. That's when I knew the truth. Because no one sounded like that going into a nest full of vipers.

No one.

Xander thought he was doing such a great job; he thought I didn't know what he was up to. There was no way that I saw him look at his watch—no way at all. It was impossible that I knew he was keeping something from me, and that his 'something' had to do with our trip into Devlin's den of evil. What Xander was forgetting was that I was much smarter than the average bear. He seemed to have momentarily forgotten about my improvements—or maybe he just didn't realize what I could really do—like smell his agitation when he started to sweat. I could see his pupils dilate when he lied—or tried to, anyway.

Yet the most interesting thing was the device I could hear on him as it quietly beeped and whirred with an electrical hum.

I smiled in the dark. "Alright. Let's go."

He pulled out some small bolt cutters he had in his back pocket, and we quickly sprinted to the fence, staying low to the ground. While he cut through the metal, I kept my eyes on the guards. They still stood nearly 60 feet away, behind a telephone pole that stood just outside the perimeter. I surveyed the surroundings, still positive a guard would come running up and fire a few rounds into our heads.

A few minutes later, Xander had cut a nice break in the chain link for us to get through. He went first, then I followed, making sure to fit the links in the fence back together so our entrance wasn't visible. Timing the security cameras, we silently ran across the twenty-odd feet that it took to get to a small loading dock area just around the back. The guards never saw us.

Under the cover of darkness, I paused to lean against the concrete side of the dock. I rested my head, laying it back against the wall and closing my eyes for just a second. I called out to Michael.

So far so good.

You're inside? His reply was fast. *That was quick.*

Not quite. We're outside one of the loading docks out back.

Oh, well, close enough. Any trouble?

I didn't want to tell him about Xander. Not yet. *Not anything I can't handle.*

You sure?

Positive. I heard footsteps coming across the dirt, just around the corner to our right, and I opened my eyes. Xander heard them, too and looked at me expectantly. *I have to go.*

Okay. Let me know when you get out of there.

Will do.

I love you. Remember—call me if you need help.

I will. Love you, too.

I mentally signed off. Gesturing to Xander, I motioned for him to stay off to the right, deep in the shadows. I stood where I was, letting the guard see me.

When he came around the corner, he stopped in his tracks and whipped his gun up to aim at me. "Who the hell are you?"

"Oh, come on..." I let him hear how exasperated I was. "You don't recognize me?" I held out my arms, kind of like a 'take a closer look,' and waited for a response, but he just stared. "Girlfriend of the Messiah? That ring any bells?"

"Get on the ground, face down!"

"Now that's no way to treat a special guest of your head honcho."

"On the ground! Now!" he barked.

I took a deep breath and sighed—but then I took another, because he smelled yummy. This guy was definitely human, definitely nervous, and had a heartbeat that could outpace a greyhound. That heartbeat also told me that he was trigger happy, and I didn't feel like getting shot today. Even so, I had to test out my abilities, right? *Might as well.*

I casually took a step forward. "Why don't you put away your gun, huh? You don't really want to shoot little ol' me, do you?" I put on my best pout.

"Stop moving and get down on the ground!" He began breathing more erratically.

Another step. "But I'm just a girl! What could I possibly do to a strong guy like you?"

"If you take a single step closer, I'll shoot you."

"Then you're going to have to do it, cause I'm stepping." One more step.

So did he, firing a warning shot near my feet. "I mean it! Stay where you are!"

"But I just can't."

As I took another step forward, a number of things happened at once. I heard a beep from behind me, and then a click in the distance behind the guard. Before I could blink, a bullet pierced his throat, his blood spraying me. Instinctively, I licked my lips and felt myself grow stronger.

The guard fell to his knees, grabbing his throat and gasping for air. Without thinking, I lunged forward and grabbed him by the shoulders. I shoved my face into his throat and inhaled the scent of his blood. My teeth changed into little white daggers as I licked the sweetness from his neck. Before I could stop myself, I bit down and began to drink from him, fresh juices pouring down my throat and satiating me like no food ever had before.

Eventually his body realized he didn't need to fight anymore. The guard stopped moving, so I released his throat. He fell forward, his arms pinned underneath his own dead weight. I stood up and wiped my mouth off on the back of my sleeve, uncaring about appearances. He knew who I was, what I was. He might as well see what it looked like firsthand. I shook myself out a little and pushed my hair back out of my face.

"You going to tell me who it was that shot him?" I asked.

"Sniper," said the voice behind me, much more serious than before.

"Were they supposed to be aiming at me?" I inquired casually.

"They were watching you, but only for my protection. Their target is Devlin."

"Good answer."

"It's the truth."

"Ah, now we're getting somewhere." I turned around and faced him. "Thanks for joining our regularly scheduled program, already in progress, Xander."

He glared at me.

I knew it had to be something like this: Xander was a spy.

"Which one is it?"

"Huh?"

"Which agency do you work for?"

"The Feds."

"Makes sense. They would be the ones most interested in a cult. Is that what this is about?"

"It was," he said, "until you and Michael brought up this vampire-demon shit."

"Of course," I replied caustically.

I realized that no one had come running for the guard despite his shouting. Peculiar but not, considering I was expecting this to be a trap set by Devlin. I looked around, and the other guards had disappeared.

"We're in for some trouble," I said quietly, still surveying our surroundings. Xander nodded in agreement. He proceeded to carry himself more like an agent now, weapon out, aiming with the professional accuracy of a trained marksman as we began moving around to the exterior of the office.

Still, no guards.

I climbed up a steel ladder to the rooftop. Xander followed, and we breached the office quickly through the ductwork. I went first, ready for an onslaught of bullets or fire, but there was nothing. I sensed *nothing*. Xander right behind me, we made our way into the office space, dropping down from the ceiling. It was dark, and I couldn't hear anything except frightened, muffled breathing.

Kat.

I found her duct-taped and bound to a chair in the corner. Her blue dress was tangled and torn, dirty from the time she'd spent here. I quickly undid her bonds and whispered to her that I was there, that she was safe, and that I would be taking her home.

"Not quite, my dear."

"Ah," I said, letting annoyance fill my voice, "you again." I stood up and turned around, facing Devlin as he stood just outside the door. "I really don't like you."

Devlin smirked. "You may not like me, but I'm glad you're here. Now we can be better acquainted without Michael getting in the way." He turned to Xander. "Or you."

With a flick of his wrist, Devlin managed to smite Xander from across the room, sending him flying into a filing cabinet, papers fluttering through the air. Kat began to scream, the scream of someone who has been through horrors and simply couldn't take anymore. Her terror hit me hard in my core. I instantly fanged out and snarled at Devlin, with no control over my ability to transform into my new state of being.

A brief moment of shock overtook Devlin's face before he grinned wickedly. "Take her," he commanded, stepping backward as numerous guards overtook his position and came pouring into the room.

"Not today, Satan," I managed to growl out.

I grabbed Kat, who was still screaming, and rushed over to where Xander lay in the corner. Without thinking, I ripped off a sheet of metal from the windows and flung it at the guards, knocking them backwards. My fingers and palms were cut, but I didn't care. Grabbing the chair Kat had been tied to, I flung it through the window, turning quickly to shield my eyes and face from the breaking glass. Holding onto Xander and Kat, I moved quickly through the window and carried them beyond the perimeter.

It took me all of ten seconds.

At that moment, I glanced back to see a S.W.A.T. team beginning to overtake the building from the exterior. *These must be Xander's backup*, I thought. A voice called on a loudspeaker for the people in the facility to lay down their arms. Shortly after, I heard gunfire erupt from within and knew Devlin would have his hands full with the FBI raiding the warehouse.

I called out to Michael, and he showed up quickly in the 300M, ready to take on any guards, Devlin, or the world if it meant keeping me safe. I shoved Kat into the backseat as he did with Xander. I climbed into the front seat and off we sped into the night. We knew the shop was compromised, so we headed back to the house. Both of us were aware that his abilities to keep the property shrouded in fog were our best protection right now, but even that protection could be limited depending on Devlin's abilities.

Upon arrival at the house, he and I took care of our respective friends. Michael brought Xander into the study and laid him out on the settee. Despite a decent-sized cut on his forehead and bruised ribs—perhaps a bruised ego, to boot— he was going to make it just fine.

I wasn't so sure about Kat. She had finally quieted down and was sleeping when I placed her in what was once my room. Her body twitched, and she murmured like a mewling kitten in her sleep. I knew she had been through something I would never know; I could only hope she would recover. For now, I left her to sleep and began planning how I would tell her everything in the morning.

Chapter Nine

Everything is Real

"I've got something to tell you."

"It can't be any worse than what you've told me before."

"Actually, it can." I paused for dramatic effect. "Xander is a spy."

Michael just stared at me.

"You know—a double-oh seven, 'Hello, Clarice' kind of spy."

Still nothing.

"He's with the Feds."

"I already knew that," he replied.

"Seriously? What the hell, Mike?" I countered. "You couldn't have told me?"

"I knew you would figure it out eventually."

"I certainly did!" I exclaimed. Then a thought occurred to me, and I narrowed my vision at him, piercing him with my eyes. "Was this a test?"

"In a manner of speaking."

"How so?"

"I wanted to see if your abilities would catch on to the things he tries to hide."

I sighed. "Of course." I rolled my eyes. "You men..."

We were sitting at the infamous kitchen table, having a glass of Pinot Noir, and watching the sunset through a large picture window. Coral clouds danced behind the silhouette of black pine treetops, a golden glow cast across the maze and well-groomed landscape. Loons called out in the distance, their calls echoing from a dream, permeating the stone walls just enough to hear them. The only thing that would have been better would have been *not* having the weight of the world pressing down from above.

We had each showered and changed into fresh clothes. After having a warm mug of 'transfusion', now was the time to relax. We were simply relishing the calm before the proverbial storm. We knew it was coming, and it was in this quiet moment that we were merely 'being.' No pressure to fight anyone or anything. We were just together, simply present and in the moment, and very much in love. I held his hand in mine, enjoying this time with him and having him near me.

I leaned forward in my chair, hearing it creak with my movement. "Next time please tell me. I didn't know if this would be that *one thing* that would end your friendship with him forever. I didn't want to have to be the bearer of bad news again, either."

"I understand. No, I knew he was a spy—I've known it for years. After the Army, he was gone on sabbatical for a year or two, and when he came back, he seemed...different."

"Different how?"

Michael smiled subtly, distracted by memories of days gone by. "He used to be so lively, so full of energy. He would show up at a party and be full of jokes and merriment." Michael's smile slipped. "When he returned, that energy was bottled up. Xander could always be stoic if he wanted to, but he seemed obligated to be that way when he came back. It was like I could sense the energy still vibrating underneath his exterior. He was like a bottle rocket, ready to explode on command. I just didn't know it was the FBI's command until a year or so later."

"And of course, you picked up on his quirks."

"What, like the watch?"

I nodded. "And the other electronic devices."

"Right." Michael shrugged. "Ultimately, it just worked out. When I needed something from another country—a settee, a cabinet, a sculpture—he was also on assignment with them. I got to have my friend nearby and he got to serve his country."

Groaning came from the other room. Xander was awake.

"Let's go see how he's doing," I said, releasing Michael's hand. We both stood up and headed to the study.

On the settee, Xander sat upright. Clutching his head like it was pounding, Xander glanced up at us as we walked in the room together. He grimaced and closed his eyes.

"Hiya, partner," I said, trying to sound cheery but coming off a hundred percent sarcastic—typical me.

"Yeah, yeah," mumbled Xander. "I guess we made it out okay." He looked up at us again. "Did you tell him?"

"Of course I did."

"Great." Xander looked over at Michael. "What damage am I looking at?"

"None," Michael replied.

Confusion and relief warring on his face, Xander asked, "Why?"

"I already knew you were with the government."

Shocked, Xander leaned back on the settee. "H—how? How did you know?"

I leaned forward, placing one hand on the arm of the chair. "You have tells, sir."

"Tells?"

"Yes," said Michael. "Whether you're aware of them or not, nothing can get past us with our abilities. We notice everything."

I nodded in agreement.

Xander shook his head. "Damn," he muttered, looking down in embarrassment and frustration. After a few seconds, he looked up again. "So what now?"

"Now we need to focus on keeping you safe," said Michael. "I can't have my lover and my best friend in harm's way."

I reached over and squeezed his arm. "Aww, you called me your 'lover.'" Michael smirked at me. "I should probably figure out how I can help on that front. I don't know what abilities I have, apart from what I learned a few hours ago."

"Did we save Kat?" asked Xander.

I sighed in relief. "Yes. She's upstairs."

"Is she okay?"

"I'm not sure." I turned to Michael. "Speaking of which, I should go check on her. Are you two going to be okay down here?" Michael nodded, and I left him with Xander to head upstairs. I took the stairs two at a time, moving quickly until I was at her door. I gently knocked until I heard her tell me to come in.

I opened the door, and she was sitting upright in the bed, pillows stacked behind her and the blankets pulled up around her like a protective barrier. Her cheeks were tear-stained, and her eyes were red and swollen. Her blonde hair was tousled and shaggy, giving her the look of a poor little waif. I could tell she was still processing the events from the hours before. It would be a long time before she would be able to speak about them without shedding tears.

"Hi, Sunshine," I said, coming over to the bed. I sat down on the edge of the mattress, gently easing into it to avoid startling her. "How are you feeling? Did you sleep?"

"Yeah. I'm alright, I guess." She smiled a little for me but refused to look at me.

"Yeah? Want me to get you something? Some juice or some food?"

"No, not just yet. Maybe some water, though?"

"Sure, hon." I grabbed a glass from the nightstand and filled it up with water in the bathroom. Bringing it out to her, she took a sip from it, and then handed it back to me.

"Can I get you anything?" I asked, setting the glass down on the nightstand.

Moments ticked by before she finally glanced up at me. "Yeah. You can tell me what happened. I don't understand any of it. Why was I taken?" Her tears welled up again. "Who was that man? Why did he do those...those things...?"

I reached out and smoothed back her hair, tucking some behind her ear. I went back into the bathroom and collected some tissues for her. I slowly dabbed the tears from her face, giving her a minute to collect herself.

Handing the tissues over, I began a tale of tales. I told her the story of my dreams of Michael. I also told her that Michael was a vampire, nearly 300 years old, and that he and I were in love as only two people meant for each other could be.

She scoffed at this part, disbelieving that Michael was anything but a normal flesh-and-blood man. Kat was never much for believing in fantasy or beyond the science of things. She learned that Devlin is not what he appears, that he had taken a sample of blood and engineered it to become all-powerful and capable of much more than Michael or I knew about. That seemed to resonate with her rationale a bit more.

I also told her what Devlin wanted: to become leader of an army of vampires with supreme abilities, all based on the blood of Michael. In my explanations, I told her she was taken solely because she was my 'sister.' Devlin wanted my attention in the hopes of capturing Michael to gain access to his blood, and she was an easy way to be sure he captured it.

"And that's not the worst of it," I said.

Kat looked at me warily. "What could possibly be worse?"

"Devlin—" I took a deep breath, because saying it to her seemed to make it fully real. "He's my father."

"Holy shit. Are you serious? You can't be serious..."

"As serious as cancer. It's on my birth certificate." After a pause, I added, "And he doesn't know."

"He doesn't know he's your father?"

"Nope."

"Wow. Just... wow."

When I told her what had happened at the warehouse, she cried for a moment, but only a moment. Upon her collection of herself, I figured it was time to rip off the band aid. I explained to her who—or rather, what—I was now. Needless to say, she lost it, but only a teensy little bit.

"A freakin' vampire? Have you lost your mind?" she exclaimed, laughing a touch.

"Yes," I said, maintaining my determined expression. "I mean, no, I haven't lost my mind. But yes, I am a vampire."

"It sounds to me like you've gone off the deep end. I mean, really, you think you're a legit, blood-sucking vampire? And this asshole thinks that you and Michael are both vampires, too?" she asked. Then she laughed some more, but it wasn't funny laughter—quite the contrary. Hers was a hysterical, crazy laughter, and it scared me a little bit.

"Seriously, Kat. We are. We—are both—vampires."

"Oh, come on. And I'm the monkey king. Get the 'F' outta here," she said, pantomiming exasperation with me. "Demons and vampires. Right. Sure." But I could see in her eyes that part of her believed me, and it frightened her. She must have seen something, some demonstration of Devlin's abilities other than the bit with smiting Xander.

"I can prove it to you, but I don't want to scare you."

"Yeah, sure," she said dismissively. "Prove it to me; I dare you. I'd like to see you try that." But she scooted back just the smallest bit into her pillows.

I frowned. "Take my hand, Kat." Slowly, she stopped laughing and cautiously took my hand. "I'm real. You know me; I'm your friend, and I love you. I'm not going to hurt you."

"I know that, silly. I just think maybe you hit your head or something. There's no such thing as vampires."

"Let me show you, okay? I promise I won't hurt you. You can trust me, okay? I *won't* hurt you."

Kat nodded her head.

That said, and holding onto her hand, I opened my mouth and let my teeth elongate. I felt the tips of them with my tongue and watched Kat's eyes widen in disbelief and abject horror. She ripped a hand out of my grip and stifled a scream.

As quickly as I had brought them out, I retracted my teeth and clamped my lips shut. Squeezing her hand with my free one, I murmured, "Hey, hey, it's okay. It's just me, Sunshine. It's Celie. I'm right here. See? Nothing scary. Everything is okay." I waved my hand over my mouth and showed her my teeth were normal again.

Kat's tears began to fall again. She was distraught, so I hugged her and held her for a time, rocking her softly to comfort her. After a few minutes, she stopped crying. I felt her breathing calmly, and she sniffled.

"I think I'm okay," she whispered. I sat back and looked at her. "So... So does this mean... Everything you told me is real?"

I nodded.

"And that man...that man was real, too?" Kat sniffled again.

"Yes. And don't think of him as a man. He's not worthy of being called one."

"It was real. All of it..." she breathed. "Everything I saw..."

"Yes, sweetie. I'm afraid it was." I hated having to put her through this, but I needed information.

"Oh god..." she murmured. Her voice dropped to a whisper and she said, "Don't let him find me again. Please don't let him find me. I can't go back there."

"I promise," I said. After a minute, I added, "But I need your help to make sure of it."

Kat swallowed loudly and stared at me warily. "What... what do you need?"

"I need to know anything he said about Michael or about me. Anything he asked you. Anything he mentioned would have involved either of us."

Kat's eyes glazed over for a moment, lost in memories and deeply painful thoughts. After a time, she refocused on me. "He...he said he was going to damn us all... He said Michael would help him do it."

"That sounds about right," I replied sarcastically, rolling my eyes. "What else did he say?"

"He said that you...you were a means to an end. He was—oh god, Celie, he said he was gonna kill me if you didn't arrive in time."

"In time for what?"

"I don't know."

"Well, that doesn't bode well."

We sat together for a time before she perked up. "I did hear him talk to one of his people, though. Something about...um..." Kat's face was pensive as she tried to recall, and I kept silent for fear of spooking her. "I think... Yeah, I think he said something about attacking on hallowed ground? Do you know what that means?"

"I'll have to talk with Michael. It doesn't sound very good."

I went to stand up, but she grabbed my arm. "Please don't leave me. Not yet." Her eyes were watery again. I stayed with her, holding her hand until she fell asleep, knowing that I needed to do everything

I could to keep her safe. She had suffered enough at Devlin's hands. Whatever was coming, I didn't want her to be involved.

I headed downstairs to find the boys had a map laid out on the kitchen table. I could see Xander pointing to something on the map, Michael nodding in agreement. They were planning something, but they needed to know what Devlin had said before they could finalize any details.

I darted over and slammed my hand down on the table. Xander jumped, and Michael looked up, startled by my sudden appearance. I realized I had gone into 'quick mode,' darting faster than they could see, and he wasn't used to my powers yet. "Just hang on, guys," I said sternly. "You need to hear this."

"What did she tell you?" asked Michael, his brow furrowed.

"Devlin is planning an attack. I think he's coming to *us*."

Xander spun away from the table, making a sound of disgust. "Aww, damn. Great." He walked over to the fridge and pulled out a beer. Popping the top off, he began chugging it down.

Michael glanced from him back to me. "Where?"

"Here. At least, I'm pretty sure here..."

Incredulous, Michael insisted, "There's no way. He can't find this place."

"In all seriousness, I wouldn't bet on it."

"Why do you say that?"

"Kat told me he was talking with someone in the cult and mentioned an assault 'on hallowed ground.' If you think about it, that would have to be here."

Awareness dawning, Michael stepped back from the table and crossed his arms behind his head. In movies, this usually happened when someone realized something profound and often jarring—heavily impacting their plans or their reality of life as they knew it. In his case, I knew this meant his brain was in processing and planning mode.

Xander had stopped and was watching both of us. "What don't I know?"

Michael looked at him and brought his arms down. "It means he's *definitely* attacking here."

"But hallowed ground could be anywhere! Isn't that usually a church?"

I nodded. "Usually, but in this case, Michael here—" I said, gesturing to Michael, "—is their Messiah. His home would be the ultimate 'hallowed ground.' What better way to take him on than on his home turf?"

"Come on, man. That sounds stupid. Who attacks someone on their home turf?"

"Devlin does," said Michael. He was eyeballing the map again. "We need to get to them before this turns into an all-out war."

I stared at him hopefully. "What did you have in mind?"

"First, we need to set up traps here."

Enthusiastically, Xander chimed in, "I'm on it."

"What about me?" I asked.

"You need to keep training. Learn what your abilities are."

"I can do that," I said, devilish glee clearly written on my face. "What are you going to do?"

"I need to determine if I can call up demons to help us with this mess. Remember I told you I can't call demons on another vampire? Well, there may not be such a rule when it comes to another half-demon."

More glee. "Oh, sneaky! Hopefully it can work." I pointed at him. "Yes—definitely check that out. Meanwhile, would it be possible for you to take Kat to Ginny's home? I'm thinking she needs to be as far away from here as she can get."

Michael nodded.

"It may be helpful for her to talk with someone who's had similar experiences, too," I added quietly.

Michael reached out a hand and placed it on mine. We gazed at each other for a minute, both knowing what this fight could mean. We could end Devlin—*end him*. We could prevent what happened to Kat and Ginny from ever happening to another person again. No one would have to endure his despicable ways, there would be no cult to take in new victims, and people would be safe. The prospect was all the encouragement we needed to get the job done.

It turned out getting our jobs done was the easy part. We each set out to work, throwing all of our anger, fear, and frustration into getting each task done, and done right. Xander proceeded to work on defenses, installing a perimeter warning system that included hazard lights, security cameras, and trip lines. He set this up in the library, which I turned into the war room. (We needed a base of operations, right?) The room held a map of the property, the perimeter system, and the weapons that we had gathered together. Heading out into town, Xander had obtained surveillance images of various abandoned buildings, including discovering a new hideout for the Sons and Daughters. These images were interspersed with various close-ups of people we believed to be in charge within the cult, and I scattered them all over a board in the war room.

Xander also spent a fair amount of time out back at the shooting range, practicing his marksmanship. The FBI had trained him well. His knife skills were also on point, and he taught me a few new moves using Krav Maga for close encounters. It was useful to have him as part of our team, even if he didn't quite grasp the severity of the situation.

I discovered I had many new abilities, some like Michael's and some different. I already knew that I could dart fast like him, but I tested it, determining my speed at 50 yards per second. Hopefully that would be fast enough to avoid bullets and other weapons, including Devlin. I couldn't invade dreams, though. That was a disappointment, as I thought I could overwhelm Michael with some spicy, late-night imagery.

However, I learned that I could shapeshift.

Yes—*shapeshift*.

This discovery actually happened by accident. I fell asleep, taking a nap in the sitting room. I began dreaming...yet it was no ordinary dream. While I slept, my body changed, writhing and stretching into that of a panther, dark and sleek, relaxed and outstretched as if on a tree limb. Michael stumbled upon me in this shape and shouted, waking me up. I awoke in this unique state, unaware that I had transformed, but still able to 'speak' with Michael using our mental connection. I remember he approached me slowly, his countenance full of hesitation, but I didn't attack him. The panther I had become was fully within my control. He guarded me as I twitched and stretched, willing myself back into my own form.

I was nude when the reverse transformation was complete. Naturally, we took advantage of it, Michael quickly stripping down until he was naked. I reached for him and pulled him close, loving the feel of him against me, bare skin against bare skin. He was warm and tantalizing, a perfect example of masculinity and spices—and he was all mine. I gasped as he reached between my thighs, and I reached for his cock in response, stroking him until neither of us could take the teasing one moment longer. We made love on the floor, rolling around on that plush oriental rug I had thoughts about weeks ago, wringing every last drop of ecstasy from each other.

Thank goodness Xander didn't walk in on us.

Michael did take me on a trip to the hospital to collect some blood. The hospital nurse, a middle-aged woman with frizzy red hair and glasses, was clearly miffed to see that he had a woman with him, being less than kind to me while still acting flirtatious with him. But who wouldn't?

I knew what I had.

The catty nurse still obtained the blood bags for us—O positive, the most common and least flavorful. We left the hospital giggling like schoolchildren, though, flirting with each other and him teasing me about my infatuation with him. Back home, he and I spent some time 'transfusing' ourselves back at the house, ensuring we were always ready for a fight and at peak potential.

In fact, we were at such peak potential that I learned blood could create quite the spicy factor for us. After I spent time lavishing attention on his cock with my mouth, he picked me up and whirled me around before bending me over the kitchen table and taking me from behind. It was rough and dirty, and I said things to him I'd never said to anyone before—lascivious, lustful, sinful things. I wanted him in all the ways only debauchery could provide. He growled in my ear and bit down on my shoulder, and the scent of my blood on his lips sent me into a frenzy.

I came three times in one hour alone.

Meanwhile, Michael proceeded to call forth favors from lower-level demons. I poked my head into his room after three days of his self-imposed isolation, finding him kneeling on the floor in a meditative state. I watched smoke float from his incense when suddenly, the smoke thickened and swirled, pouring into the space. Within a flash of dark light, an individual—tall, broad-shouldered, muscular—was standing there before him. I couldn't completely make out their face—their visage hidden by the smoke—nor could I fully understand the conversation. However, after a few minutes, there was a nod of agreement between them. As quickly as they had arrived, the being vanished, the heavy smoke disappearing with them. Michael's head bowed down in the silence.

Afraid to disturb him but needing some answers, I gently called out to him from the doorway. "Michael...?"

He turned his head to me and smiled softly. "Hi, love."

"Are you alright?"

"Yes, I'm fine. I just had a visitor."

"I saw that. Who, or should I say what, was it?"

"A demon. One of the many."

"Are they going to help us?"

"They've acquiesced and will aid in the fight."

"That's great news!" I exclaimed, then winced. "Oops, sorry," I said, this time more quietly.

He smiled. "No need. The hard part is done." He stood up from where he was sitting.

I stepped inside. "I have to say I'm surprised they're helping us—with Devlin being half-demon and all? I figured they were all about the bloodshed and chaos?"

"That they are, but they aren't happy about what Devlin has done to himself, or his desire to engineer an army of vampires. Despite their reputation, demons are purists and believe in creation the old-fashioned way."

"Oh, well, *that's* interesting. So they're jumping on the bandwagon with us. Excellent."

"Indeed."

"Alright then—we have our demons. I have my abilities, and you have yours, plus we have Xander with our defense system all set up and ready to go. What's next?"

Michael glanced down at his hands, perhaps thinking about how he would use them to kill Devlin. When he looked up, his eyes were hooded and glinting in the light. "Now, we wait."

Chapter Ten

Carnage and Chaos

The cult arrived for us on a beautiful and sunny Tuesday afternoon.

Honestly, it was like I was the girl in that classic eighties ghost movie. "They're here..." I called out to the boys, stretching out 'here' in imitation. I received no response: they were playing in the war room.

Outside, the cult had amassed in a swath of black and red, overtaking every free space from the front steps and 40 yards back. Dozens upon dozens of cult members had assembled like an emo goth concert was about to take place, and the house was center stage. I had known there were a lot of them, but seeing them all up close, gathered together to capture their Messiah and kill the rest of us—it was excruciatingly frightening.

Each Son and Daughter wore a black mask and black hooded cloak lined in red, the combination obliterating their faces from view. I couldn't tell if they were men or women, old or young; hell, there was no way to know if I even *knew* any of them. They were anonymous, faceless bodies that could be anyone—do anything—and that flooded me with fear.

There could be supervillains under these cloaks...

How did it get this bad? How did these people find leadership in a thing like Devlin Raines? Didn't they know who he was? *What* he was? I asked myself these questions as I looked out at the crowd, unable to fathom how these people had gotten this involved or how we had gotten into this position.

I shook my head, then turned and called for Michael and Xander again. I needed backup for this craziness—pronto. When both men showed up, I turned to face them.

"Listen, we need to call in the demons."

Michael shook his head. "We should wait unti—"

"No—*now*." I pointed out the window. "Does that look like the three of us are enough?"

He and Xander both stepped forward to look outside. At the same time, they both whispered, "Oh Christ."

"Take a good look out there, Mike. This is more than a handful of crazies. This is a full-on *army*." I was staring at the crowd now myself. "Those may not be vampires out there, but there are still a hell of a lot more of them than we planned for."

"Fuck, fuck, fuck," murmured Xander, rubbing his hand over his head as he focused on the intensity lurking out-of-doors. "She's right, man. There are probably—what, three? Four hundred of them out there?"

"Looks about right." Like me, Michael was staring out the window. "We need those demons."

"I'll call them. Hopefully they'll provide enough backup for us."

"Any of you see Devlin?" I was scanning the ocean of people and coming up empty.

Michael didn't search; he just placed a hand on the windowpane. "No. I don't think so: I don't feel his presence."

Xander laughed sarcastically. "I think we've got enough going on right now, don't you?"

"Please call the demons, Mike." I hoped my voice belied my nervousness. I was shaky and thought I heard it come out as I said his name. Turning to Xander, I said, "We need to get ready."

We each had our part to play in this fight. Xander and I headed into the war room and began gearing up for the attack with guns, grenades, and gas canisters. Xander wrapped his hands and wrists with tape, before putting on leather gloves. I prepped for possible shapeshifting by conducting breathing exercises and stretching. I watched as Xander donned a bulletproof vest and some simple body armor to protect himself from any gunfire that could pop up.

Mostly, this would be a Spartan-style fight, with 100-to-1 odds that simply weren't in our favor: we could be taken out by the sheer number of cult members alone. Perseverance would be the key player. Better yet, the real question was whether we would be enough. Could we survive this?

Meanwhile, Michael was kneeling in the middle of the hallway, facing the door. His eyes were closed, hands on his thighs, as he kept perfectly still. He made no sound, but I did see his lips moving.

Would this be the last time I would see him? I leaned against the doorframe and watched him. Each moment was a gift, and I savored the sight of him, my gorgeous and historic vampire—my personal hero. I stored this moment in memory, believing it would stay with me always. In my heart, I wanted as much time with him as I could get, but no, this couldn't be the end. My gut told me we were destined for more than this madness.

Smoke began to creep in from under the front door into the hallway. *Is this it?* I thought. *The Sons and Daughters are trying to gas us out into the open?* All of a sudden, Michael stopped his murmuring, stood up and turned to me. An impish smile crept across his face, and an agonizing scream reached my ears from just outside.

The demons had arrived.

"It's now or never," I said, and the three of us walked to the front door together.

Michael flung the door wide open. At first, we couldn't see anything. The smoke hung so thick and heavy on the property, it was as if the landscape had been drenched in fog, drowning everyone in a sea of clouds. Then another scream pierced our ears, and fires lit up the day in bursts of light. Roars cut through like blades slicing the air. Seconds later, the smoke began to dissipate, and the bloodshed and carnage came shining through like little rays of chaos.

The crowd had become a massive clusterfuck of hysteria. There was no rhyme or reason: mania was rampant in every part of the property, and the cult members not yet afflicted were confused and horrified. Apparently, Devlin hadn't bothered telling any of them about Michael's abilities. Maybe he didn't know? Either way, the Sons and Daughters were wailing and shouting, the scent of their fear filling the air, and black and red cloaks fluttered by as many of them ran away.

Those that remained were confronted by the demons, and they weren't as 'friendly' in appearance as they had been when I first met them. In full form now, they were frightening—nothing but elongated limbs and tails, spikes and barbs, teeth and nails. A breeze blew their stench everywhere, and it made me sick. The demons slashed and burned, tearing and ripping through the crowd like paper. Any cult members who hadn't run away were gutted, shredded, and cleaved—their bodies split apart.

It was a bloodbath.

Xander, Michael and I ran into the crowd to attack the cult members who were mad enough to fight back. Gunfire exploded from our team *and* from them. I dove for cover behind some well-landscaped shrubbery, peeking around the corner of it to fire back. My own words from my dream came back to haunt me: 'two in the chest and one in the heart.' I had some guilt as I aimed and fired back, knowing this was just a normal human being I was shooting. However, I also knew that the people who came here knew full well their goal was to capture Michael. This is what helped me to squeeze the trigger.

The crazy carnival was everywhere, gunfire sounding in spurts. Screams continued to reach us from different directions. I heard a guttural cry from behind me and spun around to find a demon roasting someone alive: flesh charred and terrified wails assailed my senses. On my right, Xander continued to fire from his position. From my periphery, I saw him throw gas canisters, followed by more blasts of his shotgun. Darting through the carnage, Michael sliced across attackers with his dagger; every single one of them tried to capture him in vain.

I had to use my new martial arts skills a few times as enemies got too close for comfort. A quick jab and then the gun, a mat soi dao (uppercut) punch followed by a te tat (roundhouse) kick. The Muay Thai that Michael had taught me was becoming increasingly valuable, and I was glad he had taken the time to train me.

Before I knew it, I was out of bullets. My gas canisters had been used, and my proficiency with the sword appeared to have been greatly exaggerated. *Must be my turn to shake things up.* I let Michael know and took a moment to breathe, focusing on my intentions. Across the way, he stopped to watch me as I stretched, writhing and elongating until my torn clothes fell away, and I was no longer human. It didn't hurt; in fact, I smiled as I changed. In a moment, I went from feeling exposed to feeling primal and alive. My black, dappled fur rippled along my spine as I shook things out. A small twitch flowed across my body just before I began moving through the crowd. My paws padded across the dirt and oyster shells of the driveway, digging in slightly as I picked up the pace from a walk to a run. I pounced on a nearby Son aiming at Michael, mauling him with my claws. I shredded his belly open, innards spilling out and the sweet scent of blood filling the air. I roared with satisfaction at the kill. Pausing for a moment, I looked at Michael, and he was watching me, beaming with pride at my outrageous ability. I chuffed for him in response.

We went on like this, attacking the many Sons and Daughters defending themselves as they tried pushing towards the house. All of us—Xander, me, Michael—were competing with the demons for kills, taking out as many as we could. Naturally, the demons had the lead on us. While a large number of cult members had run off, so many had stayed. Sometimes it seemed like as I took one down, another three came to take their place.

This was how I was captured.

I was fighting a Daughter, deep in the action, and as she surrendered to my claws, barbed netting came down over me. I roared in frustration, struggling to rake the net off of me. It was painful, piercing me all over my back and limbs. Four cult members surrounded me, and I felt something stab my left side. I roared again, calling out to Michael mentally. I heard him shout to me from across the property, his voice wild with wrath and panic, but too many of them were attacking. I flung out my paws in numerous directions, snapping and biting at the four who held me prisoner. Suddenly things grew darker, and my vision blurred. I couldn't find my legs and fell over, my chin striking the ground with a thud. I tried to look up but everything seemed so heavy.

My eyes were so very heavy...

When I woke up, I didn't know where I was. I was human again, naked, and lying in the bottom of a panther-sized cage bolted to the ground. *What day is it? What is this place?* I sat up quickly, but the drugs knocked me back down, and I found myself on all fours getting sick. After heaving for what felt like forever, the nausea subsided, and I sat back on the cold metal, trying to survey my surroundings. Was this a warehouse? It was dark, dank, and musty. Maybe it was a basement or a cellar of some kind?

That was when I heard calls from Michael. I wasn't sure how long he'd been trying to reach me, but his voice was strained with worry. Each second, they grew louder and louder.

Celie! Damn it, answer me!

Michael...?

Celie!

Please don't shout; my head is pounding.

Oh, thank God... Where are you? Are you okay? Tell me where you are. I could hear the angst in his voice, the desperation. He was more than anxious to find me, and I was more than anxious to be found.

Other than being naked in a dark and skunky place, I'm just peachy.

I was incredibly nervous about who might be watching me. There were security cameras in the corners of the open room. My eyesight was keen, so I could see there was no one else in the room with me. There was no light except for tiny red ones on each of the security cameras. I tested the bars, and they were definitely solid steel. I could move them just a small amount, the bars squealing in rusty anger at my demands, and the door of it was sealed with several locks. Oh, and each lock required a key. Yes, Devlin was better prepared for me this time. A blanket lay on top of a box next to the cage, and I reached out to pull it through the bars. Wrapping it around myself, I sat in the middle of the cage.

Hate to say it, but I appear unable to leave.

Can you tell me where you are? Do you see anything?

Not a thing except security cameras and steel bars. A possibility occurred to me, and I vocalized it. *Do you think Xander could tap into the feed somehow?*

I'll ask him. He went silent for a few minutes before replying, *He said not without knowing where you are. Did you see where they took you?*

I've been out since they captured me. I paused. *Just how long ago was that, exactly? How long have I been gone?*

Three hours.

Okay, we can work with that. I can't be that far—unless they put me on a plane somewhere? Doubtful considering the state of things. I tightened my hold on the blanket wrapped around me. The lack of temperature control, titillating conversation, and creature comforts was concerning. *I am* not *digging this place, Mike.*

I know. I'm going to work with Xander and see if we can't find an escaped Son or Daughter—one that can give us some clues.

I'm in a cage, Mike.

A cage? Fuck. Okay, let me get to work. I'm going to get you out of there, I promise.

Please hurry.

Are you sure there's nothing there to help identify where you are?

Nothing.

Ok. Please stay safe. I'll be in touch soon.

Then his mental voice was gone. I was alone again in this miserable place.

I spent some time with my thoughts—you know, contemplating existence, the expansion of the universe, why men still wear speedos... I don't know how long it was, but eventually someone showed their face. One of the cult members opened a door to my right, peering around the corner to see if I was conscious. Discovering I was, they closed the door. A few minutes later, they came back with a plate of food and a glass of water. I refused both. I wasn't hungry or thirsty—not for what they offered me, anyway.

"I'd rather die," I said as they put it on the floor. The cult member avoided my eyes and simply bent down and picked it all back up.

As they began to leave, I called out, "Where's Devlin? I want to talk to your leader!"

The cult member paused, turning their dark brown eyes towards me and piercing me with their gaze. "I'll tell him." They closed the door.

Great. Now I get to sit and wait for the dickhead to show up: what a lovely way to occupy my time.

After a moment, I began singing '100 Bottles of Beer on the Wall' because that seemed like the perfect icing to this shitshow of a cake. What was probably two hours later, all the bottles of beer were down and had been passed around. I was sitting quietly, rocking slightly to keep myself from freezing (despite my blanket), when the door creaked open again. This time Devlin himself walked in, as smug and arrogant as ever. The lyrics to Let Him Burn started playing in my head at the mere sight of him.

I hoped he could see my hatred in my eyes—my matching green eyes.

"Well hello, my dear," he said coolly.

I grimaced in response.

"Aww, come now! Is that anyway to greet your host?" he said with subtle admonishment.

I knew he hated it when I was 'disrespectful', so until I had a way out, I recognized I needed to put on a mask of politeness. "Right. Sorry. Hello! Is that better?"

"Much. Thank you for accompanying my people—"

"Like I had a choice."

"—here to my laboratory."

I was startled. "Laboratory?" I had high hopes he would wait to extract my blood until I'd been taken somewhere else, but we were already at his compound. *This is bad. This is really, really bad.*

Devlin smiled, but the devil was in the details. His teeth were gleaming but pointed, little razor-sharp rows like a small shark. "Why yes, child. I'm going to continue my work, and you're going to help me."

"I am? How's that gonna work? With you stealing my blood?"

Devlin chuckled. "It's not stealing if you just hand it over, now is it?"

"Like I'm going to do that. Just offer up my arm to you. Ha, right. No, thank you." When he focused his gaze on me, I could see the anger cutting across his features. "Excuse me. No, thank you, *sir*."

Devlin's eyes narrowed on me. "Now, you must realize, girl: you're not with him anymore—you're in *my* world. There are dozens of people here willing to sacrifice themselves on a single word from me. *You're* locked in a cage; hell, you don't even have any clothes on! What is it, exactly, that you were expecting?"

"Well, I thought you might let me go."

"Funny! A sense of humor: I like that," he murmured. Louder, Devlin said, "No. No, I'm going to take your blood and continue my research. You're going to help me create my army—*Devlin's* Army."

"If it's all the same, I'd rather not," I quipped.

"I don't recall asking you." His mouth curved into a crooked grin, his lips oddly shaped. "In fact, I don't think you have any choice in the matter."

With those words, his entire countenance transformed. His jaw began to open, popping at the hinges, and there was a cracking sound as his bones moved. His features became increasingly grotesque, manipulated by dramatic change from within. His teeth elongated, freakishly lengthening, but more than just fangs—it was *all of them*. As his eyes turned solid black, I felt my stomach turn. They were bottomless pits of darkness—shark eyes. A tail emerged from behind him, its end littered with small diamond-shaped spikes. Devlin's spine stretched, and he grew at least a foot in height, pasty white skin showing where his shirt could no longer cover his abdomen. A menacing growl tinged with fury issued forth from his throat.

He was half demon after all.

"Oh. Oh, I see," I mumbled, staring in horror.

"Do you, girl?" he snarled, the words garbled by the extra teeth in his now oversized mouth. "Do you see why you will give me what I want? Do you see why you cannot deny me?"

"Mmm hmm. Yup. You betcha."

He gnashed his teeth and grinned, an abnormal smile on a mangled shark. Gripping my blanket tighter, I heard a snap, and his tail lashed through the air, striking the cage bars. On instinct, I flung myself further back in the cage. His subsequent chuckle was a harsh-sounding noise.

"Good, girl. You're right to fear me."

I was definitely overwhelmed. How much of this was because I was alone? Or was this simply a reflex of my former self? I wasn't used to being a vampire, after all. Transfixed on him like an LSD user on a lava lamp, I watched as Devlin reverted back to human form. We were still the only people in this room: did his cult even know he was half-demon now?

Once back in human skin, Devlin dusted off his shirt, attempting a perverse smile as his jaw fitted back into place. He lurched a few steps forward and crouched down to look me in the eye. For a moment, he just stared at me, and his unreadable expression was worrisome. A moment later, he shook his head and chuckled to himself.

With a smirk on his now normal face, he said, "You know, someone once said, 'An intelligent hell would be better than a stupid paradise.'" Leaning closer, he whispered, "I knew you could be smart."

He stood and walked towards the door. As he closed it behind himself, I heard him call over his shoulder, "Welcome to hell."

It slammed shut with a clang.

"I knew I was fucked," I muttered out loud.

Just as I started to relax a little, a team of cult members came in. Most of them were in white lab coats and wearing face shields to protect themselves from contamination. Little did they know 'contamination' was exactly the end game Devlin had planned.

Bracing myself, they came and unlocked the cage, guards accompanying them with pistols pointed at me. I crawled out, holding my blanket around me. One of the guards grabbed me and wrenched it away, leaving me stark naked and exposed all over again.

"Thanks, asshole," I sneered. Frustrated, I tried not to be ashamed of my nakedness. He leered at me, grabbing his crotch while the other guards laughed.

Two of the white coats approached me and escorted me to a steel folding chair they had brought in. I was forcefully shoved into the seat, the cold steel instantly sticking to my warm flesh. I winced.

"This is so *incredibly* comfortable. Thank you."

One of the white coats grabbed my arm and began wrapping a tourniquet tightly around my bicep. A square of cotton gauze doused in rubbing alcohol was swiped across the inside of my elbow. After thumping my arm for a vein, they were handed a large needle from another white coat. Without any warning, they jammed it into my arm, affixing a tube holder and plugging in tube after tube to draw my life's blood from me.

I winced at that, too.

After a couple of minutes, they had drained ten tubes of blood from my arm. Undoing the tourniquet, they hastily removed the needle and shoved cotton gauze in its place. A white coat applied a band-aid, and then they all left, with me still stuck naked to the damn chair.

"What—no cookie?" I yelled after them. "Where's my juice?"

I was able to peel myself from the chair and hastily grabbed my blanket again. This time they hadn't put me back in the cage, so I hurriedly explored the room. I rifled through cargo containers, cardboard boxes, filing cabinets, and a desk tucked away in the back until I found some boxes with the words "EXPO-DYTE" written on them. Immediately recognizing the name of the logistics company, I reached out to Michael.

Hey, are you there, hon?

Yes, love. Are you in trouble?

Not any more than usual. Listen, I found some boxes here with EXPO-DYTE written on them. That's E-X-P-O hyphen D-Y-T-E. Got it?

I've got it. Isn't that—? That's a shipping company, right?

Yes, I said. *My boss liked to use them when she was attending a conference in Chicago. Do they have any holdings nearby? Say, within a 3-hour radius?*

Smart thinking. Let me give this to Xander. I'm sure we'll get you out of there in no time.

Thank you, but there's one more thing—and it takes precedence.

Oh?

Devlin has my blood.

Silence.

Did you hear me? Devlin has my blood now.

I heard you. Michael's thoughts were faint: this must have hit him hard.

Despite our best efforts, he's got what he needs to make an army now. We have to fix this.

I know.

What can we do? I can't fight him alone. He's definitely changed, Mike.

You've seen him?

Oh yeah—in all *his full glory. The guy is definitely a half-demon.*

More silence.

Mike? I waited. *Are you there, Mike?* Where did he go? *Honey—sweetie—you're kinda freakin' me out. What's with the silent treatment?*

Yes. Yes, I'm still here. This time, he was loud and clear. *I can't tell you our plans. There's no telling what his full abilities are at this point. We know he can get into your head, and we can't let him learn what we're up to.*

I sighed out loud. That was logical. *Understood.*

I'm so sorry, Celie. It's the only way.

I smiled. *It's okay. Really, I understand. See what Xander can learn, then* come find me.

I promise we will *get you out of there.*

I love you.

With every fiber of my being, he replied. *Always and forever.*

I knew that he meant it. We had multiple lifetimes to share together, and I would do anything to protect them all.

Always and forever, I thought to him... and then he was gone.

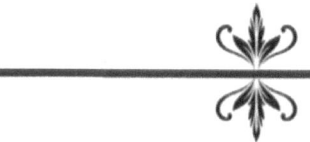

Hours passed, and then I heard it—a low rumble in my psyche, breaching the barriers of my mind. Burning cold seeped into my bones. I cringed knowing who would interfere with my body—my mind—with such intensity.

I have something for you, child.

Bite me.

Oh, I can leave that to the others. Don't you want to see what you have created?

I felt struck down. There was no way he had been able to synthesize a serum in such a short period of time! Yet, a gnawing was digging around in my gut, and I remembered that he had been working on this for years. Of course, he had everything he needed to bring about his army—all that was missing was blood—Michael's blood, *my* blood. Now he had more than enough to create the vast destruction he'd always sought.

I had to delay him: I had to give Michael more time.

Sure. Fine. Let's see what you've got, Raines.

Excellent. My guards will come to collect you.

The assholes? Okay.

He grumbled then went silent.

Six guards came in, this time all women. One of them tossed me some khaki pants and a black button-down shirt to put on—no shoes, though. I went to a corner and turned away from them, getting dressed as privately as I could. Once I was ready, I went back to where they were waiting.

A tiny girl, with short blonde hair and amber-colored eyes, grabbed me by the arm. "This way." She began dragging me, accompanied by the other five-armed women.

It still surprised me to see these people working with Devlin. How could they still be unaware of what he was? To be led by such a madman without any remorse was incomprehensible.

Leading me through corridor after corridor, we went in an elevator to the top floor of the building, which I now knew had four floors. There were windows along a concrete walkway as we left the elevator, and I could see a water tower with a name painted on it: Sterling.

We were in *Sterling*. The irony was not lost on me. Perhaps Devlin still thought that was a weapon against Michael? Still, this was good news. We were only an hour away from Bantum and just slightly more than that from Michael's home.

The guards surrounded me as we moved across the walkway, ending at a large metal door with steel bolts. One of the guards knocked then pushed it open.

Inside was the laboratory that Devlin had talked about. This was where he was at his dirtiest, his most vile. There were computers, beakers and Erlenmeyer flasks. Two Bunsen burners were lit on the table. Utility clamps, droppers and tubes, thermometers, and more were strewn about. I hadn't been to science class since high school, but 15 years wasn't long enough to forget everything that went into a chemistry experiment.

"Welcome to my laboratory," said Devlin, using the upscale British pronunciation. He was so smug, so proud of himself.

"Yup, sure looks fancy—but does it work?" I said, hoping to get a rise out of him.

"Indeed, it does, child. Indeed, it does."

The short guard led me over to Devlin and forcibly sat me down on a stool. Maintaining her handgun pointed at my side as always, she took a more relaxed stance as she turned her attention to her leader. Devlin smiled at her and gestured for her to leave. She narrowed her eyes at me, as if to say, 'Try anything and I'll end you.' Then she turned and headed for the door, the last of all six guards to vacate the experiment room.

"So what now, Frankenstein?" I quipped. "And where's Igor?"

"You think you're very clever, don't you?" he said, putting his face in front of mine. He was breathing fast, eyes wide. This was completely opposite the calm, collected exterior he normally presented. "I'm going to show you my creation—what *we* have created together."

Devlin began to roll a tube in his hand, warming it up and manipulating the purple liquid inside. I saw that he had a petri dish nearby with something that looked like a fleck of meat sitting on it. That's when I realized he was still testing human cells: he wasn't administering his serum to people yet.

He popped the top off the tube and set it down on the counter. Using a dropper, he collected some of the purple liquid from inside, then released only two drops on the 'meat' in the petri dish. Once the top was placed back on the tube, he set it down, then turned to the microscope. Using the diopter adjustment to better his view, he examined his specimen. After a moment, he looked at me, and his evil grin extended from ear to ear.

"Come." He gestured to the microscope. "See."

I hesitated then slowly slid off the stool. Cautiously, I approached the microscope and leaned down to gaze through the ocular lens.

Oh my god: he's done it.

The cells were alive. This sample of dead flesh had been reanimated. He had mastered life after death, the capability to bring those that had died back to life. There was no way to know if they were vampire cells or simply undead ones, but the implications were very real: he would have his army.

"What do you think now, child?" Devlin murmured in my ear.

I swiftly turned to my left and vomited.

Chapter Eleven

All Things are Finite

"Sorry," I mumbled. "The smell is intense."

Devlin narrowed his eyes, watching me intently. As he turned away, I exhaled with relief.

While the smell of the 'meat' was certainly rank, the prospect of what I was seeing was even more so. I had to keep delaying him: I had to keep Devlin from producing his creations. That meant going down a road I really never wanted to travel down, but desperation was driving me.

Clearing my throat, I said, "You know, we have more in common than just Michael."

Devlin said nothing. He was engrossed in the animated cells in the petri dish. I gave a little cough, and he glanced up at me.

"I said we have more in comm—"

"I heard you, girl. Stop interrupting my research." He looked back down to the lens.

I paused. I *really* didn't want to have this conversation. Taking a deep breath, I blurted out, "You haven't heard the worst of it, *Dad*."

Ah, you see? *That* got his attention. Devlin's head snapped up, and his green eyes pierced me. "What did you call me?"

Crap—I had to go full throttle into this nightmare. I swallowed hard. "Dad."

Unexpectedly, he laughed. After all this time, of all the things he could have given me, he gifted me with hysterical laughter. The half-demon, egomaniacal cult leader laughed at me when I called him 'dad.'

"Oh come now. You don't really expect me to believe *that*..." He gesticulated wildly.

"I get it. Believe me, I do," I said with all sincerity, because it was the god's honest truth. "But it's still true."

Again, Devlin smirked at me, amused and disbelieving. "This is a farce."

"No, it's not." Hesitation. "I swear."

"And just who is your mother, child?"

"Anne Moore."

Devlin looked perplexed, appearing to sink into memory. I pressed further.

"You met in the late eighties. I'm not sure where or what the context was, but I was the outcome."

Devlin seemed wary.

I rolled my eyes. "You're listed on my birth certificate."

Devlin began to laugh, only this time it was maniacal laughter that echoed off the concrete walls. His entire frame shook with the effort as his laughter overtook him. After a few minutes, he regained control over himself and faced me.

"Anne Moore..." he said, and he smiled sinfully. "And—" Another laugh. "—And you're my daughter?" He laughed again. "Today truly is a *wonderful* day."

"Wonderful how?" I wasn't expecting this reaction.

"Wonderful in that I now have a legitimate claim to this blood. *Your* blood is *mine.*"

Okay, this was *definitely* not what I was expecting. "Oh, no. No, you don't! You definitely don't have a claim to anything of mine—or me for that matter."

"Oh but I do. You are my daughter. What is yours is mine. Your blood came from me, and I'm simply taking it back."

This was a new world of shit. "No, see—you can't do that. That is *not* how this works. That's not how *any* of this works."

Devlin continued to smile gleefully, as if all the pieces of his game had fallen in place, and the future of his endeavors were now set up solely in his favor. I had given him information that I hoped would get him to back down, but instead it was spurring him forward. It would have been impossible to feel any *more* like an idiot.

"Au contraire (On the contrary)! I will take your blood, and you will be the mother of my army. They will be my grandchildren. I will call them Children of Devmoore." He reached across and attempted to touch my face, but I jerked away from him. "My child..." Then he laughed again, a wicked laugh that filled the room, and I closed my eyes.

I should have let him kill me.

An hour later, I was awakened from my sleep by Michael's voice: he was calling to me as I lay in my cage. The guards had come back for me shortly after my little exchange with Raines, and they roughly escorted me back to the basement, throwing me into my cage. The only thing I had to do was to try and rest, so I had let the silence lull me to sleep. Once I heard him, I sat up, groggy and achy from the flat, hard ground.

I'm here, Michael.

Thank God. I think we've found the building.

Good! It's in Sterling.

Yes, we confirmed that as well. We found an EXPO-DYTE warehouse and distribution center there, and Xander has already surveilled it. We think we'll be able to get you out in roughly an hour.

Excellent. I was beginning to think I was going to be stuck here with his army.

You mean—

Yes.

Fuck.

He took me to his 'laboratory' (mocking Devlin and his British pronunciation) *and showed me his research.*

And?

He might as well have whipped out his dick and whirled it around.

Seriously, Celie.

He's, he's done it, Mike. He's found the key in my blood.

Shit. I'd hoped we would have more time to stop this.

So did I.

Michael kept silent for a moment before his thoughts came through, sounding resolute. *Okay then. That's it. Today's the day. We stop him now, once and for all.*

How?

We fight.

An hour later, my mental re-enactment of The Rocky Horror Picture Show was disrupted by gunfire. I knew what that meant. I scrambled to my feet, gripping the bars in preparation for what was coming.

Michael was here.

Without warning, he was suddenly in front of me, breaking open the cage door. He held out his hand and I took it. With a newfound appreciation for the warmth of his touch, I held onto him like a boat to an anchor. Once I was out, we hugged, clinging to each other as if to say, 'Never let go.' But we had to—now was the time to fight.

He passed me a handgun and a spare magazine, then I followed him, ready to fire at the next Son or Daughter who came around the corner. We traversed several corridors before finding a stairwell and rapidly made our way up to the first floor. Xander was waiting for us.

"Long time, no see." He was firing at some cult members down the other end of the hall.

"Right? I was getting plenty of rest, but I appreciate the rescue." I was both sarcastic and grateful. Xander had put his life on the line to save me from these crazy bastards, and I was going to make him a friend for life.

"You're welcome!" he replied happily. "Now let's go kill that bag of dicks."

"Right," I said seriously. Turning to Michael, I asked, "You ready?"

"I've been ready for this for a long time," he murmured. "Let's go."

The three of us ventured out into the open, firing at will until we could get the elevator. We took it to the fourth floor, getting out and running down the same walkway as before. It already felt like a lifetime ago that the guards had led me across it. That's what major life-shattering news will do to a person—change their memories, reconstruct time itself.

As we approached the metal door to Devlin's laboratory, I grabbed Michael's arm. He turned to look at me, concern on his face. "What is it?"

"We can't let him leave."

"I know," replied Michael.

"No, it's— He can reanimate dead tissue."

"And we'll make sure we destroy all of his samples."

"But it's so much more than that. If this gets out, it's more than just the United States that'll suffer. The entire *world* will be at risk."

"That's why we won't let him leave."

"How can you be so sure?" I countered.

"I have you with me. We can do anything together." He gazed deep into my eyes, and I felt the same pull toward him that brought us together in the first place. "I believe in us, Celie. This was fate, and if it comes to it, there's no one in this world I would rather die for."

I took his face in my hands and kissed him, deep and earnestly. He responded in kind. We knew this could be the end of us, but we had to put an end to Devlin and his experiment.

"Y'all done here? 'Cause we need to run this motherfucker into the ground."

Michael and I broke our kiss to look at Xander, who was both ready to go and a little uncomfortable bearing witness to our intimate moment. I looked at Michael again, seeing his determination, then nodded to Xander.

Bursting into the room, we found Devlin was naturally waiting for us. The room had been cleared out, with no evidence of it having ever been a lab. Just a long empty room now, surrounded by concrete, there was nothing left—just Devlin at the far end, staring out the window.

I stepped into the room first. "We've come for the serum."

"I know."

"Where is it, asshole?"

"Up here," he said, tapping his temple. As if in slow motion, he turned to face us, and his eyes had gone black—dark holes boring into his skull. "You'll have to kill me to destroy it, and we both know that can't happen, *daughter.*"

Michael flinched. He glanced at me, astounded I'd actually revealed my secret, and I shrugged. I could only play the cards I had been dealt. Unfortunately, that was a hand that had gone south.

"Fine," I replied. "So we'll kill you."

Devlin didn't even blink; he grinned, though, and I've never seen anything so villainous. "Come and try it, child."

With those final words, Devlin began to transform. The three of us rushed at him, hoping we could get him in between ending humanity and becoming demonic. Halfway across the room, I began firing my gun, hoping the bullets would interrupt his changing form—no such luck. He was a shapeshifting torrent of teeth and limbs, jaw jutting outward and spine lengthening at the same time his tail grew out behind him.

Michael had darted all the way to Devlin, using his dagger to slash and stab at him. However, it was too late. Devlin was already most transformed, and his enlarged jaw snapped at Michael while his tail swished across the floor. At one point, he lashed at Michael's abdomen, the diamond spikes cutting across Michael and tearing his chest open. Grunting, Michael never slowed down, continuing to hack at Devlin's form.

I emptied my magazine before rushing at their tussling bodies, leaving Xander to figure out how to fire at Raines. Reaching them, I pummeled Devlin, hitting him anywhere he had a vulnerable spot.

But I got too close.

Devlin grabbed me by my neck and jerked me in front of him like a shield, holding my torso against him with his other hand. He screeched a loud, horrifying sound, causing everyone in the room to freeze. Realizing Devlin had captured me, Michael tried to come to me, intent on wrenching me free.

Garbled words came out of Devlin's abominable mouth. "Cease your attempts, or she dies."

Michael backed up several steps, pain and furious anger etched into his beautiful face.

"I'm taking her with me."

Michael growled. "I won't let you."

The grip on my neck grew tighter, and I gasped. Michael started forward, but he stopped as our eyes met; they were begging him to stop. He turned his gaze back to Devlin, staring him down.

"What you're going to do is let me walk out of here with her," growled Devlin with his sickening voice. "You can't stop me, and you can't stop me from taking her."

"I can try."

"It would only be in vain." He leered at him and his demon tongue—long and forked—went up the side of my face. Disgusted, I closed my eyes.

"My god, man—she's your daughter!"

"She's a means to an end—*your* end—and I'm going to take every last drop of her. She's going to be the death of you all, the mother of my children, and I will be the hero."

Michael continued to argue with Devlin, back and forth, like a snarling, verbal tennis match. I linked eye contact with Michael once, but it was long enough to convey that I needed him to continue this game of wordplay. While he kept up their back-and-forth, I focused on my abilities—my capability to stretch and shift, to change and transform.

Amidst their ridiculous alpha conversation, I did it—I shifted—but not all of me. I only needed one part—one key bit—to be altered. Sure that Devlin was immersed in their banter, I pushed my change through. Eyes closed, I felt my teeth elongate, my ears change. My jawline strengthened and shifted, and when I opened my eyes, I could see Xander staring at me with a morbid fascination—simultaneously appalled and enthralled. I strained and struggled to contain the transformation, and after a minute or two, I felt complete.

I had morphed my head into that of the panther.

As quick as lightning, I jerked my head to the left and bit down on Devlin's neck, ripping and tearing it out with my teeth. His startled look of amazement was beautiful in my eyes. He hadn't realized that I was able to make this kind of transformation.

I was like a bastardized Bastet, Egyptian lion goddess and warrior, fighting to the death against Apep the snake. I was both human and panther, feminine and feline, devastating my attacker and gaining vengeance against all of his transgressions. It was satisfying, rich and plentiful. I could feel his demon blood coursing down my throat as I shredded through neck muscles, spicy and dark like dark red wine and chocolate. This was the gift that Michael had given to me, and I was happy to use it against this odious man.

Father—would you ever know what you had given up? Did you ever consider what you could have had? Would your mind use these final moments to think about what life could have been like with me at your side?

I felt tears pushing at my eyes, but I pushed back at them: Devlin Raines did not deserve my tears, father or not.

Snarling through the blood, I felt him release me. I shoved away from him, throwing myself backward and hitting the floor—*hard*. I looked up to see him choking, unable to heal from the massive wound, and bleeding out all over his pasty skin and black clothes. Raines stumbled toward me, reaching out, but I scooted backwards, bumping into Michael. My vampire grabbed me underneath each arm and picked me up, dragging me away from the demon.

"I didn't know you could do that." Michael didn't take his eyes off the carnage.

"I'm not sure I did either. In the moment, it was the only thing I could think of to do." My eyes were also affixed to Devlin: I realized I no longer feared him, no longer cared for him, no longer hated him. He was dying, and there were no feelings left for him.

In front of us, his dying body was wilting, shrinking down and sinking to the floor like molten metal. He had no voice left, his vocal cords having been ripped apart. Hissing, volatile sounds escaped his neck wounds. His tail fell off as he began to revert back to the form of a natural human, landing on the floor with a sickeningly sticky thud. Within moments, what had been a startling villain was reduced down to a withering man. His white hair was stained with blood, his face blotched purple; he no longer resembled the man I had first met. This man was no longer a threat. I could only hope that the serum in his possession was going to be destroyed with him.

Eventually, Devlin's corpse ran out of steam, reducing him to a pile of bloody muck and bones. Michael and Xander took charge and set the mound of flesh on fire, burning all traces of him from existence in a smoldering green flame. This was the only way to be sure that he was completely destroyed: no one would be able to sample him and recreate his experiments.

By this time, the Sons and Daughters had scattered from the premises. They had heard the screams heralding the death of their leader. None of them wanted to stay behind, and they fled as quickly as they could.

Xander, Michael, and I headed back to the house. Upon our arrival, Xander disembarked. He had reports to write up regarding the cult. We bid him goodbye, but not forever. We both knew we would see him again—sooner rather than later.

Meanwhile, Michael and I took some extra time to love each other. We showered together, letting the hot water and steam heal our bodies while we healed each other's souls. I used the shower as an opportunity to explore every inch of Michael, muscles glistening and slick beneath my fingers. My hands slid from his shoulders to his pectoral muscles, feeling the strength in his chest, finding little scars and remnants from his previous life. I sighed as he kissed me, strong and deep, his hands gliding down my back and cupping my behind. I wrapped a leg around his thigh and pulled him in closer, feeling the length of him against me.

That did it.

There in the shower, he picked me up. I wrapped both legs around his hips as he settled me onto his cock. He pushed me up against the shower wall, and the cold tiles chilled my hot flesh. He drove into me, thrusting again and again as I rode him into a frenzy. We came as one, with me biting down on his shoulder and him shouting my name. I breathlessly whispered his name in his ear, and he shivered.

We dried off and moved to the bedroom, virtually repeating ourselves in desperation as we couldn't get enough of each other. Hours later, we were asleep in each other's arms. I knew I wanted to be there always, be with him always, and nothing could keep me from him... I could hear his heart beating in his chest, fresh blood having given him new life. The beating lulled me to sleep.

I woke up in the early morning hours—yawning and stretching—feeling relaxed as only Michael could make me. The room was still dark, and I reached out to thank him for such a wonderful evening.

He wasn't there. That wouldn't normally be cause for alarm, but I quickly noted the feel of the sheets was strange, and the room smelled different. I froze and then turned to my left to flip on the side table lamp, desperate to see my surroundings.

Oh no...

I was in my old room, in the old apartment with Kat. There was no Michael. There was no house built from ancient stone. There were no silken sheets and fireplace.

I popped up and grabbed a robe, quickly encasing my frame and tying the sash tight before running out and down the carpeted stairs. I reached the bottom and confirmed that yes, I was back in the old apartment.

What the hell was going on?

"Kat!" I yelled, calling out for her, knowing full well she wouldn't be in this apartment.

My test failed.

"Babe? You okay? What's wrong?" Her voice came from upstairs.

Oh my god... "Uh, nothing!" I called out.

That's right, nothing—nothing was wrong. I was only bereft of my true love. I was only back in my old apartment as if nothing had happened.

I ran back upstairs, bumping into Kat.

"Where have I been the last few weeks?" I asked her.

"What? You've been here, and at work. Why? What's going on with you? You feeling okay? You're acting kinda strange..."

"So I haven't been away? Like Vegas or anything?"

"What? No." Kat looked at my face, concern and confusion warring on her own. "Do you want me to take you to the doctor?"

"It's okay, Kat. Just go back to bed," I mumbled. I went into my room and quickly got dressed, throwing on jeans and a green tunic top. Zipping up my brown boots, I grabbed my keys and wallet from the dresser and made a beeline for the front door.

Outside, I found my SUV parked in my normal spot and hopped in, starting it up and shifting into reverse. I had to go see if this was real—I was *desperate* to see if this was real. There was no way the last six weeks of my life were simply a dream. Shifting into drive, I peeled out of the parking lot. I remembered where Michael's house was, and I began driving. I didn't care how long it took or who I would have to run over to get there—I needed to see for myself if it existed.

Had this all been my imagination? It couldn't be. No—that was impossible. Everything had been so real.

Everything.

I drove on without stopping. I couldn't stop. The entire drive my thoughts were consumed with memories: memories of him, of us, of demons. I remembered Xander's disbelief, Kat's tear-stained face, *Devlin...* How could none of that be true?

As soon as I turned onto the drive leading to his gate, I noticed everything looked the same. The trees, the woods, the road twisting and turning as it should. *This is encouraging.* The gate appeared, looming larger than life in front of me. The house was hidden just beyond, so I couldn't see it, but everything else was the same.

I'm almost home.

I entered the gate code, and it was accepted. Exhaling, the gate doors opened wide to accept me. I drove through the entrance, hearing the telltale sign of the doors closing behind me.

Driving up to the house, everything was the same: the steps, the fountain, the tower—all of it was exactly where I remembered it to be. Parking the car, I scrambled out of my seat, slamming the car door. Eager to get to the house, I ran up the front steps.

Is he home? Will he know me? Is my memory of another life with him just a fabrication? Is this just a figment of my imagination?

I took a deep breath and knocked on the front door. In no time at all, I heard movement inside, and the doorknob began to turn. The door swung open, and there stood Michael, as warm and made of flesh and blood as ever.

Shock was written all over his face; however, I could also see hope and relief in his eyes.

I didn't hesitate. As my breath left my lungs, I asked, "Do you—do you know me?"

A seductive smile grew on his handsome face, and a glimmer of fangs left me weak in the knees.

"Hi, love. Welcome home."

SHANNA ROBILLARD

FINIS